RAISING A TRUE WINNER

Tanuja Sodhi is a well-known nutritionist, motivational speaker and author of *Parenting in the Age of McDonald's*. She is an ex-Indian Navy officer from the first batch of women officers. She is a mother to a 21-year-old boy, which gave her the much-needed shove and licence to write books on parenting. She has been a wellness expert and blogger with acclaimed parenting portals like parentune.com and momspresso.com. She has Master's degrees in Business Administration and English Literature, a fellowship in Nutrition, and is a certified fitness instructor. When not at her writing desk, she can be found running marathons, participating in triathlons or trekking in the mountains. You can find her at tanujasodhi.com and also her Facebook page Wellness Hub by Tanuja Sodhi.

Also by the same author:

*Parenting in the Age of McDonald's:
Raising the Fast-Food Generation*

RAISING A TRUE WINNER

IGNITE THE BEST IN YOUR CHILD

Tanuja Sodhi

Published by
Rupa Publications India Pvt. Ltd 2019
7/16, Ansari Road, Daryaganj
New Delhi 110002

Sales Centres:

Allahabad Bengaluru Chennai
Hyderabad Jaipur Kathmandu
Kolkata Mumbai

Copyright © Tanuja Sodhi 2019

The views and opinions expressed in this book are the
author's own and the facts are as reported by her which
have been verified to the extent possible, and the publishers
are not in any way liable for the same.

All rights reserved.
No part of this publication may be reproduced, transmitted,
or stored in a retrieval system, in any form or by any means,
electronic, mechanical, photocopying, recording or otherwise,
without the prior permission of the publisher.

ISBN: 978-93-5333-608-0

First impression 2019

10 9 8 7 6 5 4 3 2 1

The moral right of the author has been asserted.

Printed at HT Media Ltd, Gr. Noida

This book is sold subject to the condition that it shall not,
by way of trade or otherwise, be lent, resold, hired out, or otherwise
circulated, without the publisher's prior consent, in any form of
binding or cover other than that in which it is published.

To my mother:
We were deprived of the beautiful essence that our relationship was meant to blossom into. We need another lifetime to rekindle our connection. I miss you and yearn for your love!

To my father:
Your tenacious prodding helped forge me into a resilient being.

CONTENTS

Introduction ix

1. Emotional Growth 1
2. Social Skills 27
3. Intellectual Growth 42
4. Active Play 81
5. Character-building 96
6. Nutrition 118
7. Inner Calm Through Mindfulness 142
8. Life Skills 149
9. Detriments of Helicopter Parenting 167
10. Self-care for Parents 178

Acknowledgements 183

References 185

Introduction

'The trouble with learning to parent on the job is that your child is the teacher.'

ROBERT BRAULT, AUTHOR

Scenario 1

'Didn't you hear me the first time I said no? You fared badly in your midterm test. So, no, you're NOT going on the school trip with your classmates. End of discussion!'

Shamefaced and crestfallen, Shaurya left the room, while his father went back to the conversation that he was having with two business associates in their living room.

Shaurya is 12 years old and doesn't have a mother. He is often punished for mistakes, big or small. There's a general aura of dread and anxiety palpable in the house whenever his father is around. He is growing up to be an introvert and a socially awkward child with hardly any friends. His school grades have been falling consistently and, of late, he has started lying a lot to save his skin.

Scenario 2

'Ok, ok, Myra…please don't throw yourself on the floor! I WILL buy you the Barbie Bubble Mermaid TODAY! Now, will you PLEASE finish your homework?'

Myra is 8 years old. She is a 'precious baby', born after eight years of her parents' marriage. She is thoroughly pampered and her smallest wish is her parents' command. Sleeping on time means chocolate chip ice cream as bribe, and a tantrum thrown by her is likely to get her a Bubble Mermaid! Her parents can't bear to see her cry, and want to avoid all confrontations at any cost. She is stubborn and throws tantrums at the drop of a hat. There are no rules and boundaries set for her at home. She is often watching TV late into the night, has a truckload of toys that fills two rooms, and eats junk food at irregular hours.

Scenario 3

'This is shocking, Vihaan! What have we not given you? We paid so much to get you into the best school in the city, let you have all the freedom to go for nights out with your friends, and never said no for money! I'm not sure where we went wrong.'

Sixteen-year-old Vihaan stands there stupefied and expressionless. His eyes are bloodshot and he's unmoved by his parents' tirade. Vihaan has failed to make it to the next grade and his parents have also just discovered that he's been under substance abuse for a year now.

Both his parents have been too busy with work and socializing, and have had no time for him. If they want to show they care, they simply give him money to do as he pleases. In the absence of parental love and guidance, he has become wayward and has been ignoring his studies. He is detached and has terrible mood swings. Now, they're taking him to a drug rehab centre.

The three situations given above may have made you cringe in apprehension. Did you wonder, what if my child turns out to be like, or is already like Shaurya, Myra or Vihaan?

Your parenting approach can decide whether your child grows up into a happy, content and successful individual, or someone who is unhappy and unprepared to handle life's numerous challenges. While other forces too will influence your child's personality over a lifetime, you and you alone will play the most pivotal role during the crucial early years to help build a rock-solid foundation for your child and mould their overall personality through unceasing love and guidance.

If you're guilty of having done it wrong in some areas so far, I would say that it's never too late to make a U-turn to get on to the right path. In writing this book, it has been my sincere endeavour to assuage most of the common parental woes by curating and offering easy, practical and effective strategies for successful parenting. Since the first eight years of a child's life are the foundational years and, hence, crucial for their physical, cognitive and socio-emotional development, this book is meant especially for parents with children up to eight years of age. I have also strived to make this book a ready reckoner for the freaked-out-and-going-nuts parent, the ever-so-curious-to-get-more-tips parent, the I-have-just-no-clue-please-guide-me parent, and I've-been-goofing-up-please-rescue-me parent.

> *'Raising kids is part joy and part guerilla warfare.'*
>
> —ED ASNER, AMERICAN TV ACTOR

Parenting, in my view, is a rollercoaster ride: part exhilaration and part anxiety. It is not just about nursing the baby, cleaning their poop, placing soft kisses on those cotton-candy cheeks and enjoying baby babble! I'm sorry if you're a first-time expecting mother and I just burst your bubble of happiness. All the activities mentioned above are definitely a part of the utter joy of being a parent, but there really is so much more to parenting. It is nerve-wracking at times, making you feel like you've been thrown into a deep pool without a single swimming lesson. There are bound to be numerous confounding moments in this adventure called parenting, when traditional sources of advice may not always suffice to help you sail through the myriad situations that life throws at you. These are the situations where you may yearn for prudent and practical guidance to help you navigate through choppy waters. It is at junctures such as these, that this book will play a vital role by throwing you a lifebuoy to help you reach shore safely!

As someone rightly said, 'Kids don't come with an instruction manual.' Also, every child is unique. So, while this book has been crafted from my personal experiences, inputs from parents who have handled a multitude of situations, and extensive research, it is possible that it may not be able to answer every possible question that a parent may have. Hence, you're surely going to need a little something more than just this book to sail you through all your parental trials and tribulations, and that something is your inherent parental instinct backed by common sense.

When I had my baby a little over two decades ago, I was precariously sailing in the same boat that many parents may find themselves in today, apprehensive that it would capsize any time. My parenting path was also a heady mix of rocky trails and smooth, flat highways. I steadily morphed from a clueless and often-at-my-wits'-end mother into a capable parent who managed to stay on track with periodic course corrections. The guiding lights in my parental transformation were a mother's instinct, some intuitiveness, trial and error, and the advice of other mothers who appeared to have greater parenting astuteness than I did. I not only survived but thrived with the right ammo in my parental reservoir, and am a very satisfied mother of a 21-year-old. I feel that if I knew what I know now, it would have made the journey much smoother. We gave our son the roots to grow and anchor himself to the correct foundational habits, and have now released him from our safe haven so that he can spread his wings and soar high in the sky to find his own place in this world and become a winner!

WHO IS A WINNER?

Is she the one who wins every possible academic accolade at school? Is he the one who wins almost all the sports trophies at school and is even playing for his state? Or is he that young man who excelled at almost anything that he attempted as a student and now has bagged the most coveted job that his peers would jump through hoops to get? I think these profiles are just too lopsided to qualify for the winning child's title. This is because we only analyse their lives from a single dimension and do not have visibility on how they have fared in other salient aspects of their lives.

A winner, to my mind, is a well-rounded child who grows up to be a happy, confident, caring, diligent and an independent adult. They should be successful in their own unique way, and not necessarily conform to our conventional definition of success, which means excelling in academics with the singular aim of landing a great job, having a hefty bank balance, a few big cars and a palatial house that the world would envy, or being an athlete at the national level who can make a profession out of their talent that will make them rich and famous.

Now, every child cannot excel in academics or a sport or a creative domain in life. In a class, there can only be a single topper; similarly, there can be only a few high-flyers within each sport. This definitely doesn't imply that these children are the only winners we have, and all the rest who don't fall into these 'elite' categories, are just run-of-the-mill. To clarify, an academic achiever may be successful in the conventional sense of the word, but may not necessarily be a happy child or adult. He may not be physically fit or may not enjoy what he is doing, he may not be sensitive or empathetic towards other people, he may not be nurturing his relationships, and so on. On no account can I call this person a winner. And then, if you look around you, not every class topper you know would have grown up to be super successful and happy in life.

A winner has to be much more than just an erudite scholar, or an athlete par excellence. A winner has to be a holistically evolved person, who likes what she does and does what is truly likeable. She is self-aware, has her fundamental values in place, treats others with respect, nurtures her relationships, looks after her physical well-being and is happy being herself. This is a successful person and a winner, to my mind.

The great poet-laureate Maya Angelou's take on success sounds simplistic and yet, is very profound and insightful. She says, 'Success is liking yourself, liking what you do, and liking how you do it.'

It may make you wonder, 'How can my parenting style be aligned to this outlook in the highly competitive era that our children live in?' In response to this, I would request you not to obsess over just one facet of your child's development, and instead provide a conducive environment for their holistic growth that includes intellectual, physical, emotional, social aspects, and character-building. And in the process, don't bludgeon them into trying to excel in everything they lay their hands on. We should not attempt to try and raise little demigods with exceptional prowess in all domains, such as strength, agility, intelligence, speed, endurance, and so on.

How can you draw a blueprint of a human that is ever-evolving, even if you happen to be its creator and chief architect? Children are not robots that you can programme as per your desire, to meet your unfulfilled aspirations. They are fragile humans and need to be nurtured sensitively. They will flourish if they have the freedom to dream, imagine, explore and create in their own way and in their own time. Their individuality, interests and confidence could wane if we try and push them too hard in too many directions, or in a direction that they are not naturally aligned to.

Just give them enough elbow room to dabble in a variety of realms without pestering them incessantly to keep performing at an optimal level. Help them gently align themselves to a domain of their interest and watch them blossom into unique beings with distinct minds of their own. In this way, you will mould them into well-rounded individuals, and set them up to lead a happy, healthy and successful life.

You may then want to ask me, 'Is liking oneself, what one does and how one does it, enough to sustain them in this ruthless world?' My answer is that, liking and respecting oneself raises self-esteem and self-confidence; and self-esteem is the foundation of a strong character on which to build one's life. When a child loves what they do, backed with high self-worth, that's the beginning of their perennial love affair with life, and the commencement of their journey towards becoming a true winner in life. This view may sound very philosophical rather than practical, but believe me, it is anything but theoretical mumbo jumbo. It definitely requires of us to provide our children with all the vital tools for intellectual, physical, emotional, social and character growth that I have tried to delineate in this book.

So, when you experience episodes of wanting to pull your hair out and you invoke the forces above to take pity on you, stop hyperventilating: I've got great news for you! Help will be sitting on your bookshelf, just waiting to be summoned! Just pick this book up, go to the relevant chapter, and let the practical wisdom help you handle these wobbly spins on the rollercoaster to ease you off your parental angst, making the ride super fun!

This book will serve as a roadmap for constructive guidance in the realms of character-building and cognitive, emotional, social and physical growth of your child. Each of these spheres is covered in separate chapters, with a comprehensive list of practical recommendations that are worth having in your parental toolkit. The USP of this book lies in its balanced approach in bringing up your child, which is critically needed in the present times, when life is moving at breakneck speed.

The book is definitely not a one-time read as it covers every intrinsic aspect of a child's growth. Childhood spans over eighteen years. So, at different points in time, you could delve into the relevant chapters of your interest and implement the interventions that you find helpful. The insights in this book are based primarily on my experiences as a parent for the past twenty-one years, the experiences of my nutrition and fitness clients, and also on the experiences of sixty parents from cities such as Mumbai, Delhi, Hyderabad and Gurugram, whose children are between the ages of 5 to 18 years. The purpose of this survey is to present unbiased and diverse parenting perspectives of parents with children of varied ages. These interviews are interspersed throughout the book and labelled as 'Survey Takeaways'. Besides, I have also harnessed tips from books and interesting blogs on parenting. And now, it gives me great pleasure and delight to help you raise a winner!

HOW TO NAVIGATE THROUGH THIS BOOK

I've structured the book into ten main chapters to mark the critical areas of a child's growth. The last chapter 'Self-care for Parents' is especially pertinent to you, the parent, as it helps you recharge your spent energy and focus on parenting with renewed verve. Each chapter in the book, with subsections on practical solutions and essential daily hacks, will hold your hand, light up the way ahead and guide you along. All the chapters are independent of each other. They're not sequentially laid down and hence, you can read the book from cover to cover, or you have the flexibility to go to any part of the book that jumps out at you, seeking your attention. Since this book is relevant for parents with children of all ages from preschool to the young adult stage, it is not a one-time read. As you repeatedly traverse the book, I'm sure you'll instinctively figure out which parts of the book are more relevant to your child's current age. You may notice some core ideas repeated in different guises in various parts of the book, such as role modelling, communicating effectively, providing a loving environment and encouraging physical activity. This is done deliberately because these interventions are intrinsic and extremely valuable to multiple growth spheres of a child, such as intellectual, emotional and social growth.

My perspective on parenting alludes to some very acclaimed and well-proven parenting schools of thought that I revere and am deeply influenced by, as much as it is based on my own experiences as a mother.

Before you plunge right into the book, I wish to offer you what I think is the best piece of advice that I ever got: While on your bitter-sweet parental voyage, always remember that you don't need to be a perfect parent. Every parent is always a work in progress. No one can be an embodiment of perfection, neither a parent, nor a child. There is no single parenting style that can be labelled as a flawless one. You just have to do your best through your constant endeavours to help your children achieve holistic growth, to release them into the world armed with the all-essential personal virtues of empathy, diligence, integrity, honesty, responsibility and gratitude. And then, just watch them grow into decent human beings who are truly happy and make their lives worthwhile. It is akin to training a pilot and then standing back and watching them soar to great heights in the aircraft of their life, knowing full well that you gave them the best foundational training in their formative years! So, dive right in and kick-start your parental voyage armed with adequate ammo!

1

Emotional Growth

'Having a two-year-old is like having a blender that you don't have the top for.'

JERRY SEINFELD, AMERICAN ACTOR, WRITER AND DIRECTOR

EVEN BEFORE THE little fledglings can focus their eyes and gurgle their first few sounds, many modern-day parents want their children to start reading, speaking and writing much before any other child of that age they know. They don't want to lose a single minute in the race to win the 'parent of the brightest and smartest child' contest. Therefore, they sometimes force babies to focus on books, and toddlers to practise writing, even before they're actually ready! This all-consuming fixation, focused around the academic success of a child, starting at an unfairly young age, is often achieved at the high cost of impairing their emotional and social development.

Beyou.edu.au[1] describes emotional development very aptly: 'Emotional development involves learning what feelings and emotions are, understanding how and why they occur, recognising your own feelings and those of others, and developing effective ways of managing them.'

While babies can display only a few emotions, they start feeling and expressing a whole gamut of emotions all through their ensuing years. Even a newborn can express her feelings when she looks into her mother's eyes while she's being breastfed. When her mother returns her gaze lovingly, the baby feels loved and secure almost immediately. While a toddler can express a few basic emotions, such as anger, joy and fear, a teenager has the ability not only to express, but also to be able to recognize a more complex range of emotions, such as awe, anxiety, excitement, irritation, hope, frustration, pride, fear, gratitude, empathy, guilt and worry.

So, why is emotional literacy so important? This is because the emotional state of a child determines the kind of person they grow up to be, and greatly impacts how they feel about themselves and behave on a day-to-day basis. This will influence their choices, actions and conduct later in life. Children strengthen their emotional prowess through the close bond they have with their dear ones. Therefore, it's very crucial to help your child understand and deal with their feelings for adequate emotional growth.

THE BENEFITS OF HELPING CHILDREN MANAGE THEIR EMOTIONS:

- It calms them down.
- It raises their emotional quotient (EQ) and makes them empathetic.
- It ensures good physical and mental health.
- It improves their self-esteem.

The following sections delineate measures that you can take to help your child build a solid emotional foundation.

GIVE THEM THE LOVE THEY SO DESERVE

Love and care are the building blocks of an emotionally strong child. The emotional climate at home is the touchstone of the mental and emotional health of a child. A deeply nurturing environment at home can have a profoundly comforting effect on children, and can promote a feeling of physical and emotional security. Loving your child generously will not only do a whole lot of good to them during their childhood, but will also go a long way to make them an emotionally resilient and even-tempered adult. In fact, a parent can never love a child too much for it to become a negative attribute. However, parents should not confuse loving a child with acquiescing to their every demand. This amounts to spoiling them, and will result in a false sense of entitlement in them.

You can show your love to your children by following some guidelines.

Spending quality time with them: This could be within a certain time window (however short) on a daily basis, and at least one longer time slot in a week. Turn off all your distractions to spend uninterrupted time with your child. Ditch all the gadgets, such as your mobile phone, laptop and TV, to be fully with them—in body, mind and spirit. You could play their favourite board game with them, go on a trail walk together, ride a bicycle alongside or just play an unstructured game in the park with them. For younger children, even reading a bedtime story can be a wonderful way to have 'together time'. Do whatever THEY fancy doing with you. Children spend a large part of the day doing what others want them to do. So, letting children decide how to spend that special time together will make them feel loved and emotionally gratified.

Let me share my own story with you. When my son was a baby, I had massive guilt trips for not being able to spend enough time with him. I was an officer in the Indian Navy and had MBA classes in the evenings. One day, when I saw my baby hanker and whine for my attention as I was leaving for work, I decided to trade weekday tasks, such as socializing, shopping, and watching movies and TV for two hours of undivided time with my baby every single day. Over the next three years, I played with him, let him ride piggyback on me, took him to the park, laughed aloud at his juvenile jokes, played catch with him and his friends, and did whatever else that made him feel happy and contented. I followed this routine for many years till he grew into a happy teenager. Talking, playing and laughing together can be very therapeutic. Children who get regular one-on-one time with parents are not only less likely to have behavioural issues at school, with friends and parents, but are also mentally and emotionally more resilient.

Displaying physical love: Make sure you hug, hold, touch, kiss, rock, cuddle and baby talk with your child when she's a baby, as often as you can. Little babies feel a sense of security when their parents exhibit physical love in this manner. For older children, hugging, cuddling, placing kisses, holding hands or placing your arm around their shoulders while walking together, can really strengthen the emotional bond. You can show your love in myriad big and small ways, like picking up your school-going child from the bus stop and taking her school bag off her exhausted shoulders, hugging her when she comes back after playtime, and so on.

Many parents find it difficult to express their love for not just their partner but also the child, especially physically. While their hearts would be brimming with love for their children, everyday matters may unconsciously compel them to refrain from expressing themselves through physical action. If you feel the same, remember that physical display of your love can provide children with a deep sense of emotional well-being and comfort, and that your unconditional love can deepen their sense of self-worth. A lifetime of robust emotional growth is a priceless gift you can give to your child!

Focusing on emotionally overwrought children: Your little one may come up to you with his drawing or a play dough creation while you're cooking or busy with other chores. Ensure that you do not brush him off indifferently or speak in monosyllables while you're engrossed in another activity. Children are very sensitive and can quickly gauge your lack of interest. It can make them feel ignored and disheartened. So, display your genuine interest in whatever they are doing when they want your attention and appreciation. Even if you're really busy, take a moment, make eye contact and say something sensitive and comforting to them. It could just be: 'You have made such a colourful picture with crayons!' or 'This is such a cute mouse you've made with the play dough!' or 'I'll be right back with you in a few minutes as soon as the food is ready!' followed by a warm peck on his cheek.

Criticizing action, not the child: Don't ever belittle your children. Avoid using words as weapons. Words such as silly, dumb, idiot and stupid are discussion killers and potent enough to damage a child's psyche. These words are humiliating and can crush a child's self-esteem and self-confidence. Even sharp criticism can be internalized to make themselves feel unworthy and inferior. For instance, 'You're fat and lazy because you eat chips and burgers so often!' is a form of 'deliberate criticism', which can have dire consequences. In fact, this type of criticism can demotivate the child rather than dissuading them from something that you don't want them to repeat. Criticize the action instead: 'Burgers and chips are unhealthy foods that can make you gain weight. You wouldn't like that, would you?' Politeness never hurt anyone.

Respecting your child's feelings: Taking their feelings seriously and acknowledging them without dismissing them or poking fun at them will prevent a child from growing into an emotionally awkward individual who cannot even validate their own feelings. The more sensitive you are towards their feelings, the more the likelihood of their reciprocating and opening up to you, especially during the growing-up years.

Never comparing: A large number of parents often compare their children to others, thanks to intense competition in every walk of life. They routinely demean their children with such comparisons: 'Look at Rohan, he has scored such high marks in maths. If he can do it, why can't you?' or 'Alia is such a soft-spoken girl, you should also try to be like her.' This can prove to be counterproductive. Parents may not realize that they are generating a lot of negative emotions in their children by doing this. When another child is being built up and your child is being pulled down, it can lead to an inferiority complex by depleting your children's sense of worth. A child with an inferiority complex is a precursor to an insecure and envious introvert in adulthood. It may also end up ruining the parent-child relationship. Remember, every child is unique and will learn and reach their potential in their own time.

Not saying 'no' too often: While it is difficult for parents to completely remove the word 'no' from their daily vocabulary in the pursuit of discipline, too many 'no's can often be futile. In fact, it may become a recipe for rebellion, with a screaming match or a full-blown tantrum. In the worst scenario, too many 'no's can shatter a child's confidence. So, what do you do when you want to dissuade your child from doing something negative or when she's being unreasonably persistent on having something? Rephrase your words to give her the same message in a more effective way. So, instead of saying, 'No! Stop hitting Saina, or else I'll spank you!' you can hold both her hands and, without raising your voice, say, 'We do not hit anyone! It really hurts!'

You can help her understand her behaviour and its repercussions better when she calms down later and is in a more receptive mood. You can then explain to her why it is not good for her to behave in a certain way, and the adverse consequences of not complying. You could end the conversation with a signal to her that even if you do not endorse her behaviour, you still love her. Save your 'no's for the extreme situations only.

Showing love in funny and goofy ways: Just because you're a parent, doesn't mean you have to put up a 'cultured and well-behaved' act all the time in the presence of your child. Sometimes, behaving goofily and playing silly games with children can put a smile on their faces that says, 'I'm feeling loved'. Being a child with your child will make them feel loved the way nothing else perhaps can. You could tickle them and be tickled by them; dance along waggishly; have a funny face contest; indulge in baby talk with your toddler; sing along no matter how out-of-tune and silly you sound. And don't forget to laugh aloud at your preschooler's juvenile jokes, as laughter is a big stress buster. Just come up with whatever works for your child and makes them super happy! You will feel their happiness through their smiles, laughter and eye contact.

Survey Takeaway: Bikram Ghatak, whose son is 14 years old, invented a goofy game called 'Sandwich Sandwich' to pep up his son's sagging spirits whenever he found him being grouchy. The parents sandwich him between themselves on a couch, tickle him and smother him with kisses till he cracks up and laughs uncontrollably, begging to be 'released'. This play not only helps them bust his anxiety, but also helps them bond as a family.

Reading together: Stories are like balms for little souls. Reading out to your child is a popular way of getting emotionally closer to him. It is one of the best ways of unwinding and releasing stress for both, the child and the parent. This activity demonstrates love and togetherness, and creates strong feelings of intimacy, emotional security and well-being for the child. Reading together is relevant for children of all age groups. While a toddler may not really comprehend everything you read out to them, they are sure to feel deeply nurtured when cuddled and read out to. The sound of your familiar voice will be very reassuring to them, and will strengthen the intimate connection with you. Read out to your older children in a way that brings characters to life and kindles empathy and sensitivity in them for others, by visualizing those characters vividly.

Expressing 'I love you' in different ways: The three words are indeed magical. When you say 'I love you' to your child often, he will feel very safe and reassured in the warmth of your love. He will pose his implicit trust in you and bloom into an emotionally secure child. But, you must say it unconditionally. If your 'I love you' is linked to the performance of your child in any field, it loses its essence. Say it when you genuinely mean it! You don't have to parrot the three words of love as they are, as this can make them sound repetitive and humdrum to the child. Be creative with your words. You can even be funny if that works with your child. For instance, you could say: 'I'm always there for you' or 'I love you to the moon and back' or use any other unique style. You don't even have to always express love verbally. You could stick an 'I love you' post-it note on his lunch box, write it on the fridge with letter magnets or write the words on his room mirror with a crayon, and so on.

Not confusing material indulgence with love: This is spoiling and pampering, rather than showing unconditional love. Too many gifts every so often can do more harm than good to your child. It can make children materialistic in their outlook, behave stubbornly when not gratified and inculcate in them a sense of entitlement. Gadgets, toys and other gifts bestowed upon the child are no substitute for showing love.

Never resorting to violence as a means to discipline: This may stop a child's bad behaviour out of fear of being spanked again, but they are more likely to be physically aggressive with other children. Physical punishment gives a child the message that it's okay to hit others who are smaller and weaker than them, as that's what they understand from the way they are punished at home. Also, a child who is spanked is likely to grow up into a resentful adult. It may not only derail their relationship with their parents, but may also ruin all their future relationships. Such children may also suffer from other psychological issues, such as depression, hurt, anxiety and low self-esteem. These may lead them towards alcoholism, substance abuse and delinquency.

AVOID MARITAL CONFLICT IN THEIR PRESENCE

Experts around the world agree that children need to be shielded from persistent marital discord between their parents. Children are very sensitive and can start sensing parental discord from a very early age. The impact on a teenager or a young adult can be even more serious. They get highly traumatized when their parents make a spectacle of their incompatible relationship by hurling personal insults, indulging in verbal malice, giving a silent treatment to the partner, playing the blame game, threatening to divorce and, in serious cases, using physical aggression. The unresolved fights can really damage the emotional fabric of a child forever. They may even affect their mental health and academic growth[2-3]. Children caught in the crossfire of squabbling parents can suffer from the following consequences:

Physical Effects of Marital Conflict on Children

- It can escalate aggressive behaviour in children, as they may assume that quarrelling, nitpicking and hitting are the only ways to resolve an issue.
- Angst caused by being witness to parental fights can make

it tough for a child to focus on academics.
- Children traumatized by serious marital conflict may be easy preys of alcoholism and/or substance abuse[4].
- Children may suffer from many health ailments, such as eating disorders (bulimia and anorexia due to depression), headaches, digestive issues, weight loss or weight gain, sleep deprivation, etc.

Emotional Effects of Marital Conflict on Children

- It can cause depression that could turn suicidal in extreme cases.
- It may lead to low self-esteem and battered self-confidence.
- It can make children indifferent, withdrawn, insensitive and disdainful towards others.
- It impinges on their ability to form normal and dependable relationships with peers and others, as they emulate their parents.
- Parental fighting erodes a child's sense of security in his family.

However, even if there are serious issues between the parents, but they act responsibly to feign a truce and resolve their conflicts sensibly in front of their children, damage can be minimized. In this way, children learn that conflicts are a part of any normal relationship, but can be resolved in a civil manner.

So, as a responsible parent, it is your duty to:

- never settle scores in the presence of your child by avoiding name-calling, hurling abuses, yelling and

threatening each other;
- never ask a child to take sides, as both parents may be equally loved by them, and this could unsettle them emotionally;
- reassure your child that the fights are non-serious, and that, all is well in the family and the family stands strong, in case the conflict is not of a serious nature;
- explain to your child later that it was wrong to have lost your temper and that, this quarrel was indeed a mistake.

According to award-winning author and clinician John M. Gottman, even emotions like anger have their place, if these are expressed constructively and respectfully[5]. He points out that being a witness to arguments and then seeing them being resolved amicably is way better than never seeing them at all.

HELP CHILDREN MANAGE EMOTIONS

As children grow up from toddlers to adults, their lives scale up in the spectrum of complexity. They face new and varied situations in life which can cause a flux and flurry of emotions. It's very easy for them to feel overwhelmed and break down, if they're not well-versed in managing the assortment of feelings like anger, frustration and fear. They may react in unseemly ways by throwing a tantrum, blaming others, being hypersensitive or being temperamental. Therefore, acquiring skills to be able to cope well with their emotions is absolutely critical for the mental well-being of your child. As sensitive parents, there's an overriding need for us to first acknowledge and then validate children's feelings; help them to identify each of these; and then, guide them on how to manage these feelings effectively on their own. By doing so, you will not only calm them down, but will also provide them with a blueprint of how they can handle their emotions skilfully and in a socially appropriate manner. Here are six ways to help your child manage their emotions:

1. **Tune into your child's feelings:** When your child comes to you to discuss a situation that she finds emotionally disturbing, listen to what she says, and how she says it. You should be able to train yourself to identify these 'tight spots' instinctively by noticing their facial expressions, furrowed brows, tone of voice and change in body language. This will not only help you tune into your child's emotional state better, but will also help you to be more sensitive in your response to her unsettled frame of mind. The insights that you gain will go a long way in guiding her to manage her emotions independently.

2. **Acknowledge, accept and validate emotions:** Many a time, you may be lost in your own world, nodding unheedingly when your child is narrating a distressing incident to you. For the child, it may be a very disturbing incident, and hence, he may be banking on you to help him deal with this antsy surge of emotions. It is your duty not to disappoint him with your unmindful responses. Acknowledge and respect his feelings earnestly, look at things from his perspective, then validate his emotions with an appropriate response that shows you understand his turmoil and care for his well-being.

3. **Identify and help label what they feel:** Recognizing emotions and then assisting your child to identify and name each one of them, can go a long way in helping them to manage their feelings in healthy ways. When you acquaint

your child with the vocabulary of emotions, it makes the process of understanding emotions easier. It will help them to uncover the presence of many different emotions, and help them realize that emotions are a very normal part of life. While it's almost intuitive for children (as is for most people) to deal with positive emotions, it's the negative feelings that you really need to help them with.

So, when you find your child distraught, angry, irritable or petrified, help the little soul by asking or saying things like:

'Are you sad because Grandmother is leaving? Are you going to miss her?'

'Are you upset because Papa is travelling, and you haven't seen him in a week?'

'Are you angry because Ayaan pushed you and you fell?'

Don't forget to label your emotions too once in a while, as this lets children understand that parents (or others) have feelings too. Express emotions with words like: 'I am feeling sad because my best friend is leaving the city to settle in another place.'

Using a Feelings Chart for younger children helps them to identify their emotions effectively. A Feelings Chart shows different feelings as emojis or cartoon faces. This can help younger children and toddlers to communicate their feelings precisely, since they lack the cognitive reasoning skills to convey their feelings clearly through words.

4. **Teach Coping Skills:** Once you've helped your child name her emotions, she now needs to understand how to express them in ways that are non-detrimental to her emotional health. Children experience many stressful situations at different times in their childhood that can leave

them distraught. We then need to promptly (yet tactfully) salvage the situation before the child explodes or clams up because of an emotional overload. Gently ask her to describe what really happened to cause her emotional frenzy while patting her tenderly. If she appears to be too distraught, you could hug her and let her know that she is safe, and that you're there to help her resolve her problem. Such a compassionate approach can help children open up and share everything with their parents. But there is a likelihood of situations when we just cannot prevent troubled children from erupting in anger, fear or frustration. At such times, they might throw a fit, whine and whimper, become clingy, throw themselves on the floor and scream, hurl affronts at you, or even hit you. This is not only a test of your parental patience, but also the opportunity for you to teach them vital coping skills. So, while you may be angry or irritated at their unruly conduct, maintain your composure and let them know gently yet firmly that you don't appreciate this violence and that there are other ways of displaying frustration and anger. You can say something like: 'I know you are angry and it's okay to be angry. But I don't like it when you hit me, as it hurts. You can hit the pillow instead.'

Survey Takeaway: Ketaki Agtey is the mother of a 15-year-old girl. She recounts her own approach on handling tantrums when her daughter was in primary school, and when all conversations to soothe her frayed nerves fell on deaf ears. She would send her daughter to her room and ask her to shout aloud as hard as she could, and to make whatever noises she felt like making at that point. She insisted that her daughter not step out of her room until she was in control of herself and could talk in a calm voice. This approach, Ketaki says, worked wonders in handling temper-tantrums and establishing peace in the house.

Here are a few alternatives that you could offer to your anxious child to help them vent in an age-appropriate way:

- drawing an angry picture
- shouting out aloud
- pounding a pillow while shouting
- stomping their feet and making growling sounds
- scribbling on a paper in an angry manner
- tearing old newspapers apart.

You could teach your older children to deal with such emotions through specific mindfulness interventions, such as:

- Meditation
- Slow and deep breathing
- Journaling (a valuable channel for venting feelings which is explained in detail in Chapter 7)
- Listening to relaxing music (light instrumental/ raindrops/birds chirping/ocean waves, and so on)
- Counting up to ten to let the negative feelings pass.

Unexpressed and unfixed emotions can even lead to physical manifestations, such as headaches, fatigue, sleep deprivation and an upset stomach. By equipping your child with the critical skill to express and manage their emotions suitably, you're not only reassuring them, calming them down, helping them build positive relationships with their peers, but you're also bestowing them with a lifelong gift of stellar mental and emotional health!

5. **Set boundaries on improper conduct:** While it is extremely crucial for children to let off steam when they're emotionally

fraught, it is necessary to set limits on the inappropriateness of emotional flare-ups and their frequency. An occasional temper tantrum is normal, but regular aggressive outbursts and bouts of insolence should not be encouraged. If this behaviour is allowed to prevail, it can become a habit which is difficult to ditch. These boundaries also tell the child that it is not okay to be impolite to others and treat them with insensitivity. As parents, it's our vital responsibility to help our children emotionally unpack, without being disrespectful. However, you do need to remember that you cannot teach a child how to behave well when he is in the middle of a flare-up or feeling anxious. He cannot think logically at that juncture, and all your words are likely to fall on deaf ears. Once your child becomes calm and regains composure, you can gently explain to him that his rude behaviour and words hurt you, as you also have feelings. Convey to him in no uncertain terms that impolite behaviour is unacceptable. If the flare-ups continue unheeded, don't hesitate to cut off some privileges as an important lesson to them.

6. **Be a role model:** Children are sponges. They watch their parents closely and feed off their emotional vibes. Imitating their parents' behaviour and actions is one of the few instincts they develop and accede to naturally. So, be cautious of how you interact with people in the family. Remember, your everyday demeanour has a big impact on your child's emotional evolution. Don't lose your cool the moment your child decides to throw a tantrum. Take a deep breath or count till twenty, if that helps. Sometimes, a pat on the back or a hug may be enough to calm down your agitated

fledgling, rather than an emotional diatribe. Your show of patience and perseverance will demonstrate to them how to regulate their own emotions in an appropriate way.

Survey Takeaway: Gauri Bajaj feels very fortunate that all the love, patience and compassion that she and her husband bestowed on their twin boys started being reciprocated ever since they were 2 years old. She says, 'My biggest achievement was when I came home crying after having a bad car accident. The then 2-year-olds got me water and chocolates and hugged me. The now 8-year-olds can sense if I am having a bad day. They come and hug me and tell me it's okay, and sit with me, just holding my hand or putting their heads on my shoulder.'

Children who remain emotionally distraught with unprocessed feelings are likely to act 'out of their element' from time to time. They could face complications in their friendships, have disciplinary issues at school, have difficulty concentrating on studies or a hobby and may not be able to enjoy stable relationships in future. All these issues could create impediments in their mental, emotional and cognitive growth. By being able to deal with compelling emotions, a child can change from feeling bottled up to being able to let out stress. This can be mentally and emotionally liberating and can help them channelize their energies in a very positive manner.

COMMUNICATION AUGMENTS POSITIVE EMOTIONS

Communicating with your child (however young or old) is one of the foundational tenets of good parenting. This creates a bond of trust that is one of the leading paths to the robust emotional growth of your child and is likely to help them grow into a happy and fulfilled adult. Therefore, you have a pivotal role to play in the quality of your child's life through the communicational approach you choose to follow.

These are some guidelines for effective communication that can go a long way in making your conversations meaningful and rewarding for your child:

Listen carefully and be involved: Your rapt attention when your child has something to say to you, will let her know that you're interested in what she is saying. Your being 'switched on' at that time is much more significant than your use of words. Come to eye level and pay heed to her body language, facial expressions and tone of her voice. Maintain eye contact and nod often while hanging on to each word she utters. In this way, you can catch the non-verbal cues being conveyed, which you may otherwise miss because of her limited vocabulary. In case you notice that she is unusually quiet, ask her questions like, 'You are very quiet today. Is everything okay?'

Don't interrupt while they speak: It's very impolite to cut your child off midway through his statements and put words in his mouth. It may not only break his train of thought, but can also discourage him from sharing his thoughts with you henceforth. Therefore, be patient and let him finish speaking, even if he is incoherent, and is taking a long time to find the right words to express himself.

Respond with encouraging words: Once your child is done with her story, it's your turn to respond by saying things that demonstrate your concern for her feelings. Your response reinforces the fact that you were listening intently. You could say things like: 'Really?'/'I see!'/'Hmmm…'/'Uh huh!'/'And then, what happened?'/'Tell me more...'/'Go on, I'm listening!'/'Looks like it was a tough day for you...'/'Looks like you had a lot of fun today!'

Survey Takeaway: Ruby Singh describes what she does whenever her daughter, who is in middle school, feels disappointed about not doing as well as she had expected in competitions. 'I have tried hard to repeat a message over the years to her, that winning or losing has very little connection to her intrinsic worth as a good person. However, this level of abstract thinking does not come easily to children who are more of literal thinkers, so whenever she loses, I listen to her sympathetically, offering comfort but no advice, and let her process the disappointment on her own. Later on, when the initial surge of hurt feelings has subsided, we have a more mature discussion on the causes of disappointment and what she could do next time in a similar situation to avoid the same. I find that this helps her to separate herself from her performance, and she is able to retain an objective perspective. Once the static of unpleasant feelings is cancelled, I have seen that she finds her own solutions, and is ready to rejoin the push and pulls of school life.'

Avoid being preachy: The last thing an emotionally distraught child wants to hear is a long lecture. Children, especially younger ones, are too immature to understand the significance of a moral lecture. Avoid phrases like: 'It's the fault of your generation ...'/'I'm your mom, so I know what's best for you!'/'What do you know about life that you talk like this?'

Words like these can sound sermonic and may lead to children losing interest in the conversation. It may even deter them from communicating with you in future for fear of enduring a 'boring' verbal tirade. So, sometimes, when your child comes home from school in a bad mood and complains about an issue with a teacher or a subject he finds tough, and then throws a tantrum, do not stand in judgement on his behaviour. Just listen and acknowledge. In such situations, children just need to unpack emotionally and they want you to help them unwind just by being a good listener. Once the emotional tide recedes, or may be later in the day, you could broach the subject, and give your opinion and suggestions.

Never use cuss words or verbal insults: However annoyed you may be with your child, avoid using insulting language. Words like 'stupid', 'duffer', 'idiot', 'dumb' and 'bloody' have a belittling effect on a child's self-esteem. Such negative language can be very damaging for their emotional growth.

Ask children about their day: While you must talk to your child about everyday things, it is always best to be specific. For instance, ask about her school and friends. When you ask her sensitive questions, listen patiently and try to help her understand why others behave differently, and how she should deal with them in a positive and affable manner.

Help children open up about social squabbles: Your love and regular conversations should help your children trust you enough to treat you as their confidante. Their trust will open doors for you to be able to gently and sensitively guide them on how to address and resolve social conflicts on their own in future. Therefore, prompt your child to share his day with you. Listen to him patiently till he finishes speaking. Help him untangle his issues in a non-judgemental way. And if you realize that he was at fault, do not pounce on him or reprimand him.

Let some time pass and maybe later in the day or the next day, urge him in a supportive way, to put himself in the other child's shoes and ask him questions like, 'How would you have felt if Ria (or whoever it is) had done this to you?' This approach will not only prompt him to understand how his negative behaviour could affect others, but will also help him resolve social issues on his own steam in the future.

Survey Takeaway: Rupinder Bhinder says that when her 9-year-old son comes to her to settle his social brawls, she first listens to her son's side of the story patiently without interrupting. She then speaks to the other child as well, to have an unbiased view of the situation. After she has established whose fault it is, she gently admonishes the child at fault, explaining to both of them how their actions could hurt other children. And finally, she makes the child at fault apologize to the other, makes them both shake hands and prods them to be friends again.

Include children in family discussions and decision-making: This approach will give them a feeling of inclusiveness and indicate to them that their opinion matters in the family. Being a part of family discussions will also open their mind to the fact that other people can have points of view that may be different from their own. That's how children learn to respect others and act responsibly in social scenarios.

Plan a family meal each day: Having a meal together as a family is much more than just a meal. It offers a great opportunity to share the day's experiences and hold general conversations. It can be an amazing stress buster for children, as they can relish the much-needed love and attention from the most important people in their lives.

If you remember to incorporate these markers into your day-to-day conversations with your child, you're headed in the right direction! It will not only strengthen your bond but will also enhance their self-confidence to form positive relationships with peers and others throughout their life.

REVIVE THE JOY OF CHILDHOOD

The ruthless pace of modern life is robbing children of their playful years, all too eager to fast-track their childhood and transform them into mini adults. Parents and schools have humongous expectations from these little beings, which is an implicit demand on them to grow up much faster than nature intended. The number of children falling prey to anxiety and depression because of this insensitive push forward, is appallingly high. It may lead to low self-esteem when they fail to achieve these goals and they may become fearful of being perceived as failures by their parents.

In this day and age, preschoolers are being tutored academically so that they can crack the 'entrance exam' for the sought-after preschools; 6- and 7-year-olds are being enrolled for serious sports coaching according to their parents' understanding of which sport their aptitude lies in; eighth grade onwards, children are being trained professionally for coveted engineering entrance exams. While children should be playing freely with no care in the world, they're being diagnosed with serious spinal deformities caused by heavy-duty school bags that hold truckloads of books and binders for homework. However, there are some ways in which you can ensure a stress-free childhood, just like you had. These are:

Free play: Children are their happiest selves when they're in the midst of free play, because there are no predetermined guidelines that dictate the play. They can imagine and create with ease, and explore the world around them without fixed-to-the-minute timings, sans the fear of being judged for their prowess or the lack of it. The play may be improvised and totally off-the-cuff to suit the mood. Children need this unorganized and flexible free play to help them loosen up from their pressure-packed schedules. When stress levels are lowered, their emotional health soars.

Free play could include a multitude of activities such as outdoor play, pretend play with dolls, toy cars, superhero figurines, music, hula hoops, blocks, playing with open-ended toys like blocks and cardboard boxes, and so on. This 'just about anything time' should be made imperative for children on a daily basis, taking them off all gadgets and their daily grind (more details on this in the Unstructured Active Play section of the 'Active Play' chapter).

Exposure to nature: Today, a regular day in a child's life is filled to the brim with scheduled activities that hardly leave any free window for them to step out of the house for free play. Added to this is the fear for their physical safety, as parents can't always be around to keep watch over them. What you get is a childhood reared in the confines of concrete structures. This, you must know, comes at a great cost. Children cannot grow into happy and free-spirited beings without a generous dose of exposure to nature. Nature indeed is a powerful healer. It helps children relax and unwind because there are no binding guidelines for them to follow in this space. Children can explore freely, prance around, run, climb, laugh and squeal in joy. These activities alleviate stress and agitation in a big way. Spending time in nature is even known to lower anger and aggression, and increase feelings of positivity and well-being. So, help children experience unbridled joy in the heart of nature (more details on this in the 'Active Play' chapter).

Survey Takeaway: Ruby Singh echoes this view, and emphasizes the need for children to be exposed to nature as one of the ways of unwinding and keeping negative emotions under check. She says, 'For years, we stayed close to a large park filled with trees and flowers, and the extremely scenic beauty and the relative isolation left a deep positive impact on my daughter's mind as she absorbed the charm of nature. She now seeks a sense of calm in the lap of nature than in the din of noisy metropolitan cities.'

Peer interactions: Friends are a very important part of children's emotional development. Just as free play and exposure to nature are therapeutic, peer interactions too are emotionally restorative for young ones. Having friends and enjoying healthy interactions with them can provide emotional security and a sense of belonging, apart from helping children to unwind. As a parent, you can play a very vital role in helping your child develop meaningful peer bonds by providing social opportunities to your child in the form of play dates, regular free play with friends in the neighbourhood park, etc. You can also nurture a few gratifying friendships of your child. Make sure you regularly encourage your child's interactions with her best friend or a group of close friends, even if it comes at the cost of sacrificing some time from your busy schedule to facilitate this. This will not only make your child very happy, but will also help her stay connected to her good friends (more details can be found in the 'Social Skills' chapter).

Letting them be: As modern parents, we have our own pressures, and seldom realize that we may be having unreasonably high expectations from our children. This desire for bringing up a 'perfect child' often leads to a very unhealthy emotional state. The never-ceasing but ever-increasing pressure can put a big dent on a child's sense of self-worth, inevitably causing stress, and leading to angst and depression. This deflated emotional state can manifest in the form of falling grades at school, lack of interest in other activities or could take a toll on their health in the form of headaches, stomach aches, sleep deprivation, eating disorders, nightmares, and more. The need of the hour is to stop putting undue pressure on children so that they don't balk under the pressure of school, homework, sports coaching, tuitions, gadget play, errands and other obligations that easily fill up all the twenty-four hours of a day. Many children jump from one activity to the other without much pause between the two, to allow them to process their experiences and emotions. Some steps you could employ to ease your child's overloaded days, are to:

- cut down screen time in favour of free play;
- slash a couple of activities from the day to help your child breathe easy and redirect focus to some other more important and interesting ones;
- reduce the heap of their toys to just a few favourite ones. This can reduce physical and emotional clutter.

Basically, turn the button for perfectionism 'off', hit the 'pause' button on their lives, and let them just be!

2

Social Skills

'24/7 once you sign on to be a mother, that's the only shift they offer.'

JODI PICOULT, AMERICAN WRITER

WHAT EXACTLY IS SOCIAL DEVELOPMENT?

THE SOCIAL DEVELOPMENT of a child is as crucial as physical, cognitive and emotional growth is to their well-being. Social development is a child's ability to understand the feelings of others while with them, and the competence to manage and control their own feelings and behaviour when they interact with others. Their interactions and behaviour with others are the governing factors of how they form various emotional connections like friendships and other relationships in life. As they interact with others, they also learn the skill of self-expression that helps them to communicate appropriately within these relationships, keeping the other person's feelings in mind. The moral and social values and knowledge that they gain from their key influencers (parents, caregivers and teachers), and what they observe and absorb from their immediate environment (peers, media, etc.), are the key drivers of their social growth. With the knowledge that they gather through these moral and social values, and the expectations that key influencers have of them, they build a sense of who they are, where they fit in the social world, how they should treat others and what their social responsibilities are.

The social beliefs of children are hugely dependent upon the answers to these questions:

- How happy is their childhood? Are they being brought up with love, compassion and positive communication?
- Are they being exposed to a lot of inappropriate and negative information through the media without supervision from adults?
- What are they being taught by their parents about how to treat others?
- Do they have friends to play with or are they reclusive?
- How do they see their parents and family members treating other people?

PARENTS ARE THE KEY INFLUENCERS OF A CHILD'S SOCIAL GROWTH

There are many influencers in a child's social growth, such as parents, teachers, peers, extended family, family friends, sporting groups, other social groups and the media. Through daily contact with most of these, the child learns about the social world around them, the social practices and the existing value system. However, parents remain the first and the most prevalent influencers in a child's social development, as in most other areas of their growth.

A child's social growth begins immediately after birth, when you baby talk and your baby gurgles back in glee, you make eye contact and the little one's eyes gleam in joy, when you clap, hug, place soft kisses on his cheeks and he wiggles in sheer delight. Through such everyday interactions, your baby is building his first emotional connection with you, the first person in his life. He is learning to put trust in his relationship with you, and also developing his social skills, though in a very juvenile way.

BENEFITS OF SOCIAL GROWTH

Forming lasting and meaningful friendships: When there is a lot of meaningful and healthy communication every day within a family, children get to learn these skills and use them with others. They discover the art of interacting with others and learn to overcome their social anxiety and awkwardness.

Developing language skills: Interacting with parents, teachers, peers and other people, and hearing them talk, help children to learn new vocabulary and enhance their language skills.

Bolstering self-esteem and self-confidence: With improved language skills comes self-confidence, which in turn helps children to mingle easily with other children and make friends. This gives a boost to their sense of self-worth.

Building empathy: When children receive a lot of love and affection from their close circle of people, and observe them treat others with compassion, they too learn to treat others with respect, fairness and empathy.

Building positive and enduring relationships: When children are raised with a lot of love and care at home, they tend to have a high EQ, which helps them value and invest positively in each relationship. And these relationships can help them navigate through anxious moments as a child and as an adult in the future.

Creating individuality and handling conflicts: When children get ample opportunities to interact with other children and adults, and have a good circle of friends, they get a sense of who they are in relation to others. This feeling of being a distinct individual helps them to carve out a strong personality for themselves.

Dealing with emotions: This is extremely important for a child's well-being. A good social growth gives a child a platform to express their emotions appropriately. This ability to manage their emotions can help them avoid behavioural issues, equip them to deal with challenges and to overcome emotional roadblocks. This ability can also help them manage and avoid conflicts with peers effectively.

Having now realized how crucial a role social development plays in a child's overall growth, as custodians of our children, we should do everything in our power to help them evolve socially. The ensuing sections lay down important interventions that can help children immensely in their social growth.

NURTURE THESE BUDS AND WATCH THEM BLOOM

When children receive love and nurturing from their parents, they learn to trust them, besides, of course, being enveloped in a sense of emotional security, belongingness and physical safety. They then instinctively learn to love and respect others, for they've seen love in abundance around them. And when they learn to love and treat others with respect, they're more likely to form strong, positive and lasting relationships in life. Keeping a close watch over their social activities, mood, behaviour and social media activity is part of showing your love. This will ensure that there is no strong negative influence around them and that no one is bullying them or exerting negative peer pressure on them.

THE POWER OF LITERATURE AND THEATRE

I distinctly remember studying Moral Science as one of my subjects during my primary school days. The textbooks had short and simple stories with a moral value highlighted at the end of each story. And I can still recall vividly that I looked forward to these lessons at home too, especially because of the way my mother read them out to me. That was one great way to introduce some basic values into a child's life. Moral Science may have become 'obsolete' today and gone off the syllabus of most schools, but the need for young children to be taught these values hasn't lost its relevance. Today, these values are needed more than ever, and the onus is heavily on parents to impart these life-altering values to their children. Here is how you can inculcate moral values in your child without being preachy:

Experiential teaching: Experiential teaching happens through teachable moments. A teachable moment is an unplanned real-world opportunity to impart wisdom. These moments can present themselves at any time. For instance, when your little one witnesses another child crying and sitting in a corner, and narrates the incident to you, you can make this a teachable moment. You could ask her questions like: 'Why do you think Rohan was crying today? Do you think he was feeling hurt because the other children were not playing with him? Or do you think he was feeling ill?'

After she thinks and comes up with her idea on why Rohan cried in school, you could take the conversation forward meaningfully, by further asking: 'Could you have helped him in any way?'

Questions like these will encourage your child to think about other people's feelings, empathize with them and perhaps, think of age-appropriate ways of chipping in to improve their situation. Seize 'teaching moments' like these to impart social values, such as:

- respecting others
- being compassionate to people in need
- appreciating people from different cultures, with different skin colours, from different strata of society or with learning disabilities.

Playing board games: Games such as Scrabble, Monopoly, Pictionary, Connect 4, and Snakes and Ladders will not only augment the knowledge base and communication skills of children but will also provide opportunities for them to act in ways that will impact others besides themselves. These multi-player games simulate various scenarios and are testing grounds for situations where your child:

- has to share her toys with other children, which can teach her to be generous and considerate;

- has to wait for her turn while others are taking theirs, which can teach her to be patient and cooperate with others;
- may not always win.

Reading stories with social lessons: Reading stories together can be a subtle yet a very effective way of imparting values to your child. Read out stories about friendship and other relationships through popular storybooks, such as: *The Giving Tree, Jataka Tales: The Wind and the Moon, Panchatantra: The Four Friends and the Hunter, Aesop's Fables: The Lion and the Mouse, The Rainbow Fish* and *How Full Is Your Bucket? For Kids*. Such books and fairy tales help teach social values to younger children in an interesting way, without sounding too didactic. After reading out the story, involve your child in a discussion about what their opinion is about certain actions in the story, and how they would have reacted in a similar situation. The social lessons that these storybooks aim to teach children are:

- How to resolve day-to-day social conflicts effectively.
- How and why should children put themselves in other people's shoes and think about others.
- Why and how they can be compassionate, caring, respectful and fair.
- How to be courteous when they meet others.
- How to make friends.
- Why they should listen to others' opinions and show interest in what others do.
- Why it is good to appreciate and compliment others.

Teaching good social values to children can have far-reaching effects in their lives, as acquisition of good values is a harbinger of good conduct in life.

WALK THE TALK

Parents and the immediate family are the first points of contact and also the first role models for children to learn about social relationships. 'Walking the talk' is one of the most potent tools in your arsenal to help children imbibe social ethics and etiquette, rather than giving a stiff moral lecture. They will watch you 'do' and then try to mirror your behaviour. We must generally be circumspect about how we behave with others in the presence of our children. Remember, the tiny pair of peepers may be watching you, and those teeny-weeny ears may be hanging on to every word you utter to others!

Here are a few ways of modelling positive social behaviour for your children:

Words are powerful, use them judiciously: If your child hears you use negative or swear words for the family or to describe others often, he is sure to mimic you someday by hurling them at someone else. Remember, you're being heard!

Be respectful while interacting with outsiders: Treat other people with warmth and regard. Take your child out with you on errands and display small acts of kindness and courtesy. Let him see you hold a door open for a senior citizen; let him hear you say 'Thank you' to the lift operator and watchman. He is learning how to value and respect other people by watching you.

Survey Takeaway: Gauri Bajaj and her husband always greet their colony guards and home support staff very warmly. Their 8-year-old twin boys have been observing their parents' polite behaviour towards others very keenly since a very young age and have imbibed the same humility. It is therefore no surprise that the boys too always wish the guards and their domestic helps every day, without being prompted to do so.

Respect diversity: Be appreciative of people who are different from you. In your conversations about others, show respect for people from a different culture, with a different skin colour, different looks, different religion, from different strata of society and people with special needs. In this way, you're modelling empathy for your child.

Socialize with friends: Help your child enjoy healthy friendships and other relationships in life by being a model for them to follow. Make time to nurture your own friendships and be a caring friend. If you're sincerely invested in your friendships and you're there for your friends when they need you, your child learns how to treat their friends well too.

Exhibit good social etiquette with others: Greet people warmly when you meet them. Smile and say, 'Hello', 'Please' or whatever salutations need to be used when you meet someone. Teach your child that it is important to greet people warmly in a customary manner. Some children are shy and initially hesitate to comply. Do not repeatedly force your child to wish a visitor, thus embarrassing her in the guest's presence. However, continue teaching her the importance of good social etiquette and politeness, and let her watch you extend social courtesies to others consistently. She will come around eventually.

Admit your mistakes: Another example of good role modelling for the virtue of fairness is, when you goof-up sometimes as a parent (parents are human too), you shouldn't be ashamed to acknowledge your mistake, and apologize for it. By accepting your fault and apologizing to your child, you're demonstrating that you respect your child's feelings and you're honouring your commitment to honesty and fairness.

Always remember! Teaching by demonstrating exemplary conduct is much more effective than lecturing, screaming and threatening children to comply!

DESIGN REAL SETTINGS TO PRACTISE VALUES

All the home lessons and role modelling to teach social skills can come to nothing if children are not provided with real-time social scenarios and experiences to practise these skills. Children need to connect face-to-face with other children of their age to form relationships and grow into healthy social beings. As part of our parental responsibility to facilitate their social growth, we need to seize social opportunities for our children, and if these are inadequate, design a few social settings to encourage social interactions. This is even more important in single-child families.

Make unplugged outdoor time mandatory through the following social settings:

- Group outdoor active play, such as: free play in the backyard or playground, neighbourhood cricket and football, day hike, Four Squares and Hopscotch
- Group board games, such as: Chess, Monopoly, Pictionary, Scrabble and Uno
- Play dates with other children, at your place or by sending your child over to a friend's place
- Birthday parties
- Summer camps
- Hobby classes like aerobics, beadwork, clay modelling,

carpentry and orchestra
- Picnics with other children or families of friends to a botanical garden or to any open area where children can run around and play
- Organized outstation hikes/treks with other children
- Organized visits to museums, zoological parks, historical monuments and art galleries
- Social and cultural functions
- Hosting other children along with their families at home
- A weekend getaway or a short vacation with friends who have children of the same age group

Following are the benefits of the scenarios listed above:

- Children learn to share—be it toys, games, books or space
- They get to know other kids and make friends
- They enhance their communication skills by conversing with others outside their homes
- They learn to care, empathize with others and respect their feelings
- Stress is released when they laugh, have fun and unwind with other children
- They get new opportunities to explore, imagine and create
- They learn to resolve conflicts on their own, which can help them be more independent
- In relation to others, they learn about their individuality

SCREEN TIME AND SOCIAL DEVELOPMENT

In this age and era of smart phones, a major chunk of a child's time is spent with their heads buried in a screen, either watching

TV, playing video games, surfing the Internet or texting and updating their status on social media. I'm not exaggerating when I say that many children in this tech-era would have learnt to swipe the mobile screen long before learning to hold a crayon. I remember a funny baby video I once watched: A 1-year-old was given a storybook that he tried to swipe in vain, assuming that is how everything works, and got increasingly frustrated at his failed attempts. It was really cute to watch, yet sad to imagine the wider repercussions of screens on tender minds.

Social skills today have been linked mostly to how many viral messages one can share on WhatsApp, how many people one can chat with simultaneously, how many friends one has on their Facebook friend list, and how many 'likes' their profile pictures and posts garner. Face-to-face interactions are shockingly on the wane as children are found glued to their screens in their leisure hours. This has stretched thin the social fabric of the present generation and social media is beginning to cast its spell even on children of a very tender age.

It is pertinent to mention that these screens cannot be branded as out-and-out villains, as they do have their utility. Computers help children research and access vast amounts of information for their assignments and other school projects with just a few clicks of their fingertips. TV has some great educational, adventure, cultural and sports-based shows, and world news. And social media helps people connect with like-minded people and form new friendships.

The problem arises when children go overboard, spending hours and hours on the TV, laptops, gaming consoles, tablets and mobiles. They lose precious time that could be used more productively. Why just children, even adults are as addicted to their smartphones and tablets, if not more. The effects of being addicted to social media or even TV or video games on children's social growth are many. These are:

1. **Loneliness:** Much of this time could be spent playing and socializing with peers. Children miss out on all the fun and laughter that offline friendships can provide. They get too immersed in their screens to notice the vacuum being created around them in the absence of fulfilling relationships. Emoticons are poor substitutes for the genuine and real smiles that friends can bring to their faces.

2. **Normalization of violence:** When children are habituated to watching shows or videos that depict violence, aggression or inappropriate content, they get desensitized to these acts of violence and start believing them to be real and normal. Viewing these regularly can change the psyche of a child, leading to apathy, indifference and aggression. In worst cases, their apathy and indifference can lead them to derive sadistic pleasure out of such violent scenarios in real life too. Such children do not evolve into sensitive beings and fail to understand other people's emotions.

3. **Poor interpersonal skills:** Since these children seldom interact with others, they lose crucial opportunities to build on their communication skills, besides forging relationships.

4. **Anxiety and low self-esteem:** Many gadget-addicted children become impatient and irritable when they're implored to step out of the screen-generated stupor. They're likely to be prone to anxiety and depression, according to a study conducted by Jean Twenge , a professor of Psychology from San Diego State University[6-7]. Many feel disconnected even with their parents and immediate families. If your child

is not playing outdoors with children of his age group, then there's a high probability of them becoming withdrawn and having low self-esteem.
5. **A sense of vanity:** Social media can make children (especially teens) conceited to a large extent. They tend to gloat over online adulation while also becoming indifferent to real people around them.
6. **Becoming a victim of cybercrime:** There are many incidents of cyber bullying that have caused anxiety and even suicides, in extreme cases. There are many online sexual predators on the prowl, luring naive and unassuming children.

It is a critical need of the hour for parents to curb the time spent in front of screens to safeguard the social growth of their children.

ESTABLISH A MEDIA PLAN TO PREVENT SCREEN ADDICTION

Ration screen time: Establish limits on when, what and how much TV to watch, and other screens to indulge in. Make this diktat non-negotiable. As per the latest WHO guidelines, infants under 1 year of age should not be exposed to electronic screens at all, while children between the ages of 2 and 4 shouldn't have access to more than one hour of 'sedentary screen time' each day[8]. This is because the brain is still developing at such a tender age, and such young children are very likely to be negatively influenced. But that definitely doesn't mean that older children aren't at risk of suffering from extended screen exposure. I know of a teen in my close circle of friends who was so addicted to playing video games that he became disconnected even with his parents and turned into a social recluse. He had to undergo psychotherapy to heal.

Monitor TV content: TV shows in the present times need close supervision. Watching inappropriate content with aggression and violence, including sexual brutality, should be strictly forbidden. Encourage children to watch educational, adventure and sports-based shows instead.

Set up tech-free times and zones: Make sure the following are screen-free zones in the house:

- The TV or computer in children's bedroom(s) at least one hour before bed
- The computer in the study room during study hours (unless the laptop is required for an assignment)
- Mealtimes
- Social occasions, such as family get-togethers and having friends over.

Be a good role model: If you expect your child to take heed of your instructions to lay off screens, you need to adhere to this discipline yourself. So, if you're consistently seen with your eyes fixed on your mobile, laptop or the TV, your child will not only follow suit, but may outdo you, turning your family into a screen-obsssessed household.

3

Intellectual Growth

> *'Learning is their journey.*
> *Let them navigate.*
> *Push them to explore.*
> *Watch them discover.*
> *Encourage their questions.*
> *Allow them to struggle.*
> *Support their thinking.*
> *Let them fly.'*

UNKNOWN

THIS QUOTE BEAUTIFULLY sums up the essence of a child's learning journey. It should serve as a guiding light for us as parents, to focus on the salient aspects of our children's learning. As their foremost teachers, our teaching methodology should kindle the child's thinking, imagination and creativity. Merely focusing on the school curriculum as the major scope of our children's learning would be a skewed approach, as that doesn't hone their cognitive abilities to their full potential. We should strive towards nurturing them in such a way that children perceive, interpret and learn about things from every opportunity provided by their immediate environment.

Every child has a distinct learning curve that may differ slightly or majorly from others of the same age group, leading them to their learning milestones in different time spans. We need to accept and respect this uniqueness of a child by helping them to learn at their own individual pace, rather than by pushing them to learn faster than they can cope.

The first eleven years of a child's life are the most crucial years in shaping their intellect to the fullest, as described by Jean Piaget in his theory of intellectual or cognitive development[9].

While it is fair to expect educational institutes to fulfil the intellectual needs, parents definitely need to find effective ways to make learning wholesome.

This chapter explores ways of achieving intellectual growth and making learning effortless and fun, rather than just an obligatory chore for children. The sections in this chapter lay down vital interventions that can augment the following aspects of a child's intellectual growth:

- Perception
- Creativity and imagination
- Critical thinking
- Problem-solving and decision-making abilities
- Memory
- Attention span and concentration
- Language skills
- Visual and spatial processing

READING IS LIKE BREATHING FOR THE MIND

'One of the greatest gifts adults can give—to their offspring and to their society—is to read to children.'

—CARL SAGAN, ASTRONOMER AND AUTHOR

Reading makes learning limitless, and is one of the surest ways of helping children to think in unique ways. It's an indubitable truth that a child's reading habit is crucial to their success in academics and in life in general. It's never too early to start reading to your little ones. You can start as early as when they can focus their eyes on the images in a picture book. They may not really understand every word you say at that age, but the experience of reading to them is deeply comforting. Children can start reading, in the real sense of the word, generally from the age of 4.

Some of the benefits of reading are:

1. **Sparks curiosity, stimulates imagination and ignites creativity:** When a young child is read aloud to, it arouses his curiosity and triggers his imagination, as he can picture the story vividly in his mind. There are no real limits to conjuring up images and scenarios in a child's mind according to their age-appropriate perception. Creativity is born from this fertile imagination. Reading adventures of fairy-tale characters and fantasy realms opens doors to so many new and fantastic worlds for a child. It will help his imagination take a flight of fantasy to mythical lands. He will begin to mentally explore people, places, things and events that are outside his physical realm. He will start imagining what the characters look like, what they're capable of doing and how they go about their adventures.

Books stretch children's imagination, amplify their world and set them up for instant virtual travel. Reading is the surest way of expanding the imagination and strengthening the roots of creativity in young ones. Some works of fiction that my son enjoyed immensely during his growing-up years, are *Harry Potter*, *Artemis Fowl*, *Septimus Heap*, *Pendragon*, *Chronicles of Narnia* and *Magic Tree House* series of books.

2. **Forms an invaluable habit for a lifetime**: Initiating reading very early in life has the potential to make a child a book lover. The early reading habit helps children ease into reading independently. They don't have to then depend on their parents all the time to choose a time convenient to read together. Many children who start reading very early in life get so habituated to reading books that they even find small slices of time to squeeze in reading sessions at any time of the day. This surely is one great addiction that a parent doesn't need to worry about!

3. **Develops language skills:** Reading stimulates the part of the brain that promotes comprehension of vocabulary and language. When you start reading to children very early in their childhood, it helps them acquire language and literacy skills sooner than the rest of their peer age group. When they're read to as babies, they listen keenly, become familiar with sounds and start understanding them very early. They're exposed to a large vocabulary on varied topics, something which can't be accomplished otherwise. This is because the language of the books is more vivid and eloquent compared to everyday spoken language. Since early readers have a better understanding of language, richer vocabulary, better spelling, superior sentence formation and

more accurate grammar and syntax, they enjoy a head start in academics by scoring better, especially in literacy-based subjects over late readers. Their love of reading makes them more effective at written communication and more articulate at oral communication too.

4. **Is a powerhouse of knowledge:** When young children read stories or are read to, it rouses their curiosity about different cultures, remote places, an assortment of ethnicities, diverse people, motley emotions, and a lot more. Stories that they hear as children not only quench their quest for knowledge but also form the basis of their individual thought process, brand new ideas and a fresh perspective on life. They learn how to decipher and deal with different concepts, issues and unique situations around them through these stories. These stories help them to shape their worldview, which our day-to-day structured routine with limited surroundings cannot provide. It is books that help them escape mentally to various parts of the world, widen their horizons, gain greater general knowledge and prod them to ask questions about life. There are scores of books like *How Things Work*, encyclopaedias, picture books (on subjects like vehicles, the human body, fruits and vegetables), National Geographic books and *5,000 Awesome Facts* that are wonderful sources to quench a child's thirst for learning.

Survey Takeaway: Ketaki Agtey started reading to her daughter when she was just 6 months old, as a bedtime ritual every night. Today, her daughter is a voracious reader at 15. She was only 12 years old when she had read *Anne Frank: The Diary of a Young Girl*. She was so moved by her heart-wrenching plight that she wanted to visit the museum of Anne Frank in Amsterdam. The book left a lasting impression on her young mind and taught her a lot about the history of World War II.

5. **Boosts concentration, attention span and memory**: It is no secret that toddlers lack focus and concentration, and when they see a book, they generally have a strong urge to tug at it and tear it apart. But, hang on! It's just the initial reaction. You just need a few iterations of reading to the restless toddler before her concentration span starts to head northwards. This increase in focus and attention span at a very young age will do her a whole lot of good when she enters school. Retention and recall of information are easier for such children, compared to others who haven't been initiated into reading early in childhood.

Fun ways to inculcate reading habit in children:

1. **Read along with your munchkin**: While it's great reading out to your children, it's double the fun when you read 'with' them. Involving little ones in a story-telling exercise, makes reading a very interesting affair. One or two such sessions, and the child gets hooked on to this activity. There are many ways of pepping up these cosy sessions, like:

    - bedtime storytelling when you tuck your child into bed;
    - storytelling by singing nursery rhymes from books with vibrant pictures. Rhymes are a great way of teaching speech to toddlers because of their sing-song appeal;
    - amplifying reading sessions with a little drama. Ask your child to put up a 'pretend-play' where he acts as his favourite character from a book. You could join the act

to double the fun quotient;
- sharing board books about birds, animals, flowers and vehicles with your toddler. He would love it even more if you describe the pictures with actions;
- reading to your child from any printed material: a magazine, recipe book, newspaper, comic strip, brochure, or anything else you can lay your hands on. These add to the variety and freshness of reading. It doesn't have to be just a 'storybook' every time;
- sharing encyclopaedias, science fiction, mystery, *How Things Work* series, biographies, autobiographies, historical fiction, realistic fiction and poetry with older children according to their individual tastes.

2. **Take them to a local library or a book club:** A day out to a local library for variety and a change of scene can really infuse newness to the experience of reading a book. You should also encourage your child to visit their school library and borrow books that they like. Book clubs add to the excitement because someone else reads out to them in an animated manner with an element of drama thrown in.

3. **Allow your child to choose her books:** There'll be a stage when she insists on reading an altogether different book from the one you choose for her. It's a very normal part of her growth, as she is just starting to establish her individuality. Moreover, if your child has selected a book, she is more likely to pay attention and relish the experience when it is being read to her.

4. **Be prepared to read your child's favourite book a hundred times:** Well, almost literally! In fact, reading a story over and over again has proved to be very beneficial for younger

children. The seemingly infinite iterations may annoy you, but they help the child build strong associations with the characters therein, leading to deep emotional experiences. You may recall how, as a child, you never got bored of reading some stories or comic books again and again.

5. **Dabble with different categories of books:** If your child doesn't seem to have an interest in reading despite your earnest efforts, or if her interest in reading suddenly drops, it may be time to infuse some variety. It helps to experiment with different categories of books, such as historical fiction, fantasy, sci-fi, biography, mystery, comic books, etc. When given a wide choice of literature, even the most unwilling readers can transform into book lovers!

6. **Choose books that are vibrant for young ones:** Select books with vibrant pictures, bold and high contrast images, rhyming text (for very young children), glossy pages and big font. Toddlers and preschoolers love board books and activity books. They love vivid and exaggerated images of dinosaurs, fairies, dragons, bears, lions, etc. Older children have more distinct tastes that are based on their individuality. They're more likely to choose a book based on the genre rather than by the look and feel of the book.

7. **Make reading interactive:** When you encourage your child to express his opinion every once in a while about the characters, settings or other facets of the story that you're reading together, it will stimulate his mind, making him more enthusiastic about these reading sessions.

8. **Find new and engaging ways to encourage reading:** Sometimes, you may have to resort to completely original or unconventional ways of instilling a love of books in your

child. Some of the interesting ways that come to my mind are:

- taking your child to a park and reading to him
- organizing book swap parties with his friends
- playing games based on books
- introducing him to films based on books

Survey Takeaway: Deepa Krishnan, whose son is 13 years old, recounts that it was the exposure to film adaptations of books that hugely inspired her son to start reading biographies and books on war. She says, 'We watched a few National Geographic documentaries and feature films on World War II together, such as *Schindler's List*. This made a huge impact on him, and now he is hooked to books on war history and famous leaders.'

9. **Lead by example:** It's a given that children shadow adults. So, walk the talk! Make reading a family affair. When they catch sight of you reading regularly, they're more likely to pick a book up. Emilie Buchwald rightly said, 'Children are made readers on the laps of their parents.'

The importance of early reading cannot be overemphasized, but parents need to know that there is no fixed age at which a child may start reading. You shouldn't lose your nerve and fall to pieces if your child hasn't started reading while another child of the same age has been hooked to books for a while now. Every child has a different reading milestone, as they all develop mentally at different rates. While most children should be able to read simple sentences between the ages of 4 and 6, some others may take a little longer to start reading. It is definitely not a race, and every child will progress at their individual pace! We just have to keep making the effort to read to them, making it an enjoyable experience rather than a tedious chore.

WRITING IS A MIGHTY TEACHER

Reading and writing are the two essential pillars in the academic success of a child that give her a clear head start. Help your child hone her penmanship at an early age. It doesn't have to be something meaningful that she writes at that stage. It could just be doodling for preschoolers and writing a letter, story or a daily journal entry for older children.

The cognitive advantages of writing:

Boosts eye-hand coordination: Children start putting pen to paper by learning to scribble randomly at first. Then they move on to copying bold letters. They keenly observe the prototype letters that they're required to copy graphically, or the watermark letters they need to trace. They notice how each letter is formed, how it starts, and where it ends. This visual act of scanning back and forth, and then writing, enhances their eye-hand coordination.

Improves spellings: Evidence from studies has shown that the more children practise handwriting, the better is their spelling memory. While practising writing, children come across simple vocabulary that is repeated ever so often. These iterations help them to memorize spellings much faster than children who do not practise writing drills.

Facilitates reading proficiency: Writing by hand engages specific neural networks in the brain that are connected with the reading function. This association helps enhance the reading skills of a child who is in the habit of writing.

Enriches recall and synthesis of information: Writing by hand has been proven to help recall of information in general, and classroom notes in particular, much more effectively than typing on a computer. This is because of the fact that the related part of the child's brain receives specific feedback through their motor action (writing) that fortifies retention and recall of information.

Strategies to encourage your child to write:

Be a role model: It helps children to make writing a habit, if they observe you writing on a regular basis. This is likely to stir your child's curiosity about writing and initiate them into attempting the same.

Encourage your toddler to scribble and scrawl: Toddlers generally start their writing journey with scribbles and doodles as they're discovering the thrill of holding a pencil, pen or a crayon for the first time. Before you know it, this apparently 'meaningless writing' may transform into writing of consequence, and your little one may be hooked on holding a pen with a purpose.

Explore different mediums of writing: To make learning-to-write fun, you could let your child dabble with slate and chalk, or even a magnetic doodle pad.

Seize every writing opportunity that you stumble upon: There will be numerous occasions that would show up in the form of events, travel, excursions and festivals that you could

Intellectual Growth • 53

convert into opportunities for your child to write. Some such instances are:

- **Family vacations:** Persuade your child to write short notes about the places you visit, and what she likes about them;
- **Picnic with friends:** Encourage her to describe the highlights of the picnic on a piece of paper;
- **Favourite hobby:** Have her write a short account about why she loves her hobby;
- **Birthday of someone close:** Help her pen down her wishes in a birthday card;
- **A grocery shopping trip:** Give her the task of making a shopping list on a piece of paper, while you prompt her with the items on the list;
- **Word/thought of the day:** Form a habit of writing a 'word/thought of the day' every day as a family. While anyone in the family could come up with the word or phrase of the day, give the responsibility of writing it down to your child. And don't forget to explain the meaning of the word/phrase to her as an added benefit!
- **Remembering someone:** If your child is of the age that she can write a few sentences without difficulty, encourage her to write a letter to someone she misses. It could be a letter to a grandparent, an aunt, a friend or a cousin. This will not only help her practise the art of writing, but will also help her express her feelings well, besides of course, making the receiver of the letter feel special.
- **Maintaining a journal**: This is one exercise with multifarious benefits, very high on my list of

recommendations. This is not only a great way to practise writing, but is also a valuable channel for venting feelings (discussed in detail in the chapter 'Inner Calm Through Mindfulness')

Praise their writing effort: Dole out words of encouragement to your child when he attempts to write. This positive stroke will arm him with confidence to write more often. Some examples are: 'This is an interesting note', 'You have described your vacation so vividly.'

Don't force a child to write: When you force a child to do something that he doesn't want to, he is likely to develop an aversion to it, as he may start associating that activity with pressure and stress. So, keep a paper and a pencil near him, but never coerce. He will start writing soon.

Writing, as we can see, has numerous intellectual benefits, many more than typing. So, dissuade your little one from swapping his pen for a keyboard, whenever possible!

CONVERSATIONS WITH QUESTIONS ARE TONIC FOR THE BRAIN

Involving your child in a real conversation widens their horizon. Rachel Romeo, a Harvard and MIT graduate, puts across this thought very aptly: 'The important thing is not just to talk to your child, but to talk with your child. It's not just about dumping language into your child's brain, but to actually carry on a conversation with them.'

Answer their questions

When your 2-year-old asks you questions like, 'Where did I come from?' you may be a little flummoxed at first for not really knowing how to handle this. But do not let any of her questions go unanswered! Think and respond with an answer that is age appropriate. If you go blank looking for the right answer to such a loaded question, tell her that you're not sure of the answer and that, you will find out and revert with it soon. By asking questions, she is not trying to test your knowledge or shock you. She is seeking information to play an active role in her own learning. Her questions are helping her to comprehend how things work in this colossal world. Through this to-and-fro conversation, her critical thinking, language skills, perception and imagination are being enriched.

Children start asking questions at a very young age. The questions are not necessarily verbal at that age. A toddler is actually asking a question when she:

- touches something and feels its texture;
- picks up something and observes it keenly;
- looks at something and then looks at you quizzically;
- points at something; and
- points at something and blabbers.

At this point, you should first help her form her question clearly (that you assume she is asking), and confirm with her if that's what she is trying to ask. For instance, if she picks up an orange and looks at you, you could ask her: 'Are you asking me what this fruit is called?' Once she confirms with a nod or a blabber, answer her question. This will help her develop her language skills and assist her in forming short questions as she grows up. A preschooler will start asking short questions with a few words as her verbal skills develop. Remember not to get irritated or impatient when she asks silly (to you) questions, as every child develops language skills at their own individual pace.

Ask them questions

Asking thought-provoking questions is valuable for the intellectual growth and problem-solving ability of your child. An open-ended question is not only a smart way of helping a child think critically, but also promotes a smart use of language. Such questions have no single rigid answers and therefore, compel your child to think and formulate a verbal response with words rather than just a monosyllable or a nod. Some examples of such questions are:

- 'How did you draw this picture?'
- 'Why do you like this doll so much?'
- 'How was your day at school?'

And when you do have conversations, don't forget to use new and relatively complex words with your child to enhance her vocabulary further.

BRAIN DRILLS HELP WHET INTELLECT

Who said learning should always be a humdrum activity limited to text books and classroom sessions? There's a wide world of fun-learning that extends from right outside the school gates, and you can be (and should be) a part of it. There is a whole variety of one-on-one and group games, as well as many fun activities for your child. While one-on-one activities give you and your child unhindered time to bond, group games help children with their social growth, along with the brainpower boost.

Intellectual benefits of brain games and activities:

1. **Improves cognitive skills:** These brain-stimulating games and activities kindle logical thinking, creativity and problem-solving ability. They enable children to process sensory information that they gather during play, memorize it, evaluate it, analyse it and then recall the same when needed. Here is a list of some of these brain-stimulating games:

   - Rubik's Cube
   - Origami
   - Maths games
   - Puzzles (animals, birds, numbers, letters, shapes, parts of the body, etc.)
   - Pretend play
   - Riddles
   - Brain-teasers
   - Shape sorter
   - Building blocks
   - Chess
   - Free play with cardboard boxes and plastic containers

2. **Enriches memory:** Many activities and games employ the learning process through association technique, wherein a child labels all the sounds, emotions, things, tastes, body parts and people's names that they see or hear. This helps them to memorize all that was labelled. Some such games

and activities are:

- Simon Says
- Coin-matching
- Story-telling memory game
- Match the colours
- Flashcards

3. **Sharpens focus:** Younger children are a bundle of energy and cannot focus for long spans of time on any one activity. You could help them build their focus by exposing them to some specific games/activities, such as:

- Colouring cards
- Crossword and jigsaw puzzles
- Spot the difference
- Card games like Memory
- Statue

4. **Boosts verbal literacy:** Brain games improve verbal fluency by enhancing working memory. Simply put, these games sharpen recall, making it easy to translate thoughts into spoken words, and help retrieve the right words at the right time. Some activities/games that help children improve their verbal skills are:

- Show-and-tell
- Tongue-twisters
- Picture storytelling
- Identify the object
- Extempore

5. **Revitalizes auditory memory:** Auditory memory is the

ability to retain and recall words, numbers, phrases and other important information that one hears. Some games/activities that can help promote a child's auditory memory are:

- I Went to the Market: This is a memory-based chaining game wherein children take turns to add a new item to a list. Each child has to first recall the list of items vocalized by the previous participants, and then add a new item to the list. It starts like this: 'I went to market and bought…'
- Telephone or Chinese whispers
- Treasure hunt
- Number memory game: It requires you to make a combination of random numbers and ask your child to repeat it. You need to keep making the combinations more complex so that your child requires more focus to remember and recall these strings of numbers.

6. **Expands knowledge and word power:** Some activities and games enrich children's knowledge base. There are numerous such games made for children of different age groups. Some of these are:

- Alphabet and maths puzzles
- Word hunt with flashcards
- Scavenger hunt
- Pictionary
- Scrabble
- Boggle
- Hangman
- Monopoly
- Crossword puzzles

- Name, Place, Animal, Thing

Education along these lines can be sheer fun, with the added perk of parent-child bonding. So, expose your child to new things often, and help them satisfy their innate urge to learn new things through varied education-based games and activities.

TRAVEL WITH YOUR CHILD
TO EXPAND HIS WORLD VIEW

Travel in any form, whether it's a family vacation, a weekend break, a road trip, or even just a daylong sight-seeing jaunt, is one of the most exciting sources of learning for children and adults alike. Travel is stress-free learning, sans the anxiety associated with textbook learning. Children end up learning many lessons about the world around them in a fun and exciting environment that a vacation offers. It is education 'on the go'.

Some benefits of travelling:

Creates a sense of discovery: Travelling to a new place that they have never visited before intrigues children, as it stimulates their natural inquisitiveness, leading them to explore a new culture. And curiosity, as they say, is the precursor of creativity.

Broadens their horizons and helps them appreciate difference: Children learn innumerable things about new cultures, new languages, new people, histories of the world, foods they eat, and many other facets of their lives by just observing them. Travelling to new places and meeting new people also teaches them the importance of appreciating differences between races, ethnicities, cultures, people and thought processes.

Reboots the brain to enhance focus: A fresh environment and a stress-free mind is a great combination to foster new experiences that are absorbed and internalized by children. For instance, travelling to the mountains for a vacation or a trek can serve as a breath of fresh air (literally too) that rewires the brain, enhances focus and sharpens mental receptiveness.

Travel doesn't always have to be a journey to places far and wide. For parents who find it difficult to lay aside a chunk of time or money to plan a family vacation, some day trips too can be a great source of learning. Some ideas for day trips are:

- tour of a local museum
- trip to a city library
- trip to a farmer's market
- excursion to a zoological park
- day trip to the city's historical landmarks
- walk through forest trails/plantation
- day trip to a village with rich folklore
- day spent at a centre for performing arts
- tour of an art gallery.

All the places listed above provide opportunities for children to get first-hand experience of things that they have been reading about in their textbooks or hearing about from their parents, friends and peers.

An excellent way of reinforcing learning through travel and day trips is to review and reassess them with your children on completion of the trip. Ask them questions about the trip and listen to their responses keenly. Some questions you could ask are: 'What was the most special thing about the trip?' Was there anything educational about the experience?' 'Where would you want to go next?' These questions will help them recall whatever they would have learnt from the trip, helping them commit everything that they learnt to memory.

MUSIC IS FUEL FOR THOUGHT

An early introduction to singing or any exposure to music is known to perk up the positive centres of the brain that release dopamine (a neurotransmitter that makes us feel happy), which in turn, kick-starts cognitive development in children from a very young age[10]. Music has a soothing effect on a child's brain. It is, therefore, good to initiate children into the sphere of music as early as you can. It could start with singing nursery rhymes to them, playing music or a musical toy.

Children who are enrolled for music classes portray a comparatively heightened level of brain development compared to children who have no exposure to music. Research carried out by Boston's Children's Hospital has validated this theory. An experiment was carried out to find out what happens when children participate in music classes. This study was conducted on fifteen musically trained and twelve musically untrained children aged between 9 and 12 years[11]. The outcome of this study, as published in the online journal *PLOS ONE*, was that children with early musical training experienced advanced executive-function skills during cognitive testing. Music actually kindles several regions of cognitive development, such as language, memory and creativity.

The cognitive benefits of music are:

Aids in revitalizing memory: You may have noticed many toddlers who may not have developed speaking skills, but are quick to recognize their favourite songs and move their bodies in response. Words or language set to a tune make it easy for a young brain to process, retain and recall information much faster than when it is not in the form of music.

Enhances verbal communication skills: In the process of learning the lyrics of a song, children often sing along. This helps them decode sounds, identify words and gives them a good training in language. A few iterations of the song, and they discover how to speak the words, which then helps them with sentence formation. Then they learn the meaning of those words with the help of adults around them. Playing an instrument can further help a child improve their reading and comprehension skills[12-13].

Helps increase attention span: We all know that babies have fleeting attention spans. However, put on their favourite song or a rhyme, and watch their eyes light up in elation. Their focus instantly goes up, and you immediately have their rapt attention!

Amplifies reasoning ability: This is especially applicable when a child plays a musical instrument. A child who learns to play an instrument discovers that strumming a chord (guitar), striking with the beater (drums) or pressing a key (piano) makes sounds. He then fine-tunes his learning by identifying the differences in the sounds generated by applying different amounts of force. All these things require him to study the cause and effect of the types of sounds being created by the same musical instrument with different amounts of force. This sharpens his reasoning and intellect.

Playing a musical instrument enhances numeracy skills: Music and mathematics have a few parallels. Both are made up of patterns and sequences that fire up the brain cells. By understanding the beat, tempo, rhythm and scales of an instrument, children are more likely to figure out concepts like counting, division, ratios, sequencing and pattern-based mathematics.

Three Types of Exposure to Music

1. **Listening to music:** Let your child embark on her musical journey by listening to the rhythm and melody of songs or rhymes. Whether you sing to her (even if you're badly out of tune), or play songs and nursery rhymes to her, it's going to be a beautiful learning experience for her. Even musical toys like rattles, bells, shakers and musical cot mobiles make the grade, as babies just love musical sounds.
2. **Singing:** Most children can sing from the age of 2 years. Once you get a whiff of it, encourage your child to sing in one or all of the following ways:
   - Sing-alongs with you
   - Call-and-response songs where the leader (you) sings a phrase and the follower (your little one) sings a different phrase in response
   - Exposing her to her favourite songs while eating at home, during a car drive or as a lullaby. Replay these as often as she wants you to. Sooner or later, she will start singing.

Survey Takeaway: Sameer Roshyan has an 8-year-old son, Adi who seems to have developed an impulse to speak in verse. This became an enjoyable pattern in the household because Sameer and his wife often talk in rhymes in the presence of Adi to make the conversations interesting, and to help him learn English the fun way.

He says, 'My son's oral communication skills and vocabulary have improved substantially as a result of this fun routine. Once, when I was travelling for a day, my wife baked him a cake, which led to the following dialogue between them:

Mom: Adi, I baked a cake for you.
Son: O thanks dear mamma because I was feeling blue!
Mom: And why was it you were so sad?
Son: He's gone out of town so I was missing my dad!
Mom: Don't you worry he'll be back by night.
Son: Then I'll take for sure that sweet cake bite!

I was taken aback by this poetic conversation. We now look forward to such interesting conversations with Adi and he doesn't disappoint us!'

3. **Playing an instrument:** Playing a musical instrument is a great form of cognitive exercise. You can encourage your child to learn and explore any musical instrument you may already have at home or have access to. You could even buy an age-appropriate instrument, like a bell, shaker or tambourine for your very young child to play with. As he grows up, you could get him a miniature instrument, such as a small drum set, colourful xylophone or flute. You could always buy him a guitar, violin or any other instrument of

his choice at an appropriate age. If he shows keen interest in playing an instrument, you could consider enrolling him in a class or getting him a private tutor.

The more variations of music you expose your child to, the more new neural pathways are created between the cells in the brain. So, don't fuss and fret when your little one announces that he is going to sing, and wants you as the sole audience of his little out-of-tune 'melody'. Just sing along with the same gusto!

ART IS A WELLSPRING OF CREATIVE EXPRESSION

Just like music, some other creative arts too ignite a child's brain. They prod children to think out of the box and to come up with their own unique creations. Young children have an innate impulse to create and art is the perfect channel for them to dabble in their creative impulses. Your child could choose from a huge repertoire of art activities, such as painting, drawing, play dough modelling, pottery, sculpting, calligraphy, paper origami, stained glass painting, beadwork, sewing, tie-and-dye, candle-making and papier-mâché.

Creative arts strengthen the visual perception of a child, and this is vital for the development of cognitive abilities and perceptual aptitude.

The cognitive benefits of creative arts:

Inspires creativity through experimentation: Exposure to art gives birth to creative expression. For instance, when a child starts painting, she may be pleasantly surprised by the discovery of a new shade while mixing colours, or she may think of adding a new element to her painting that is different from the original model picture that she may be trying to replicate.

Sharpens critical-thinking skills: Since art facilitates a fresh way of thinking, it helps creative people carry out mental synthesis of a problem in a variety of ways and to generate several solutions for the same problem.

Enables visual processing: Children dabble with the visual elements of art, such as lines, colours, shapes, patterns, textures, space and forms in activities like drawing, colouring, stained-glass painting and calligraphy. These activities sharpen their observation skills and expand their perceptual aptitude (the skills that are needed to hone a child's ability to compare and visually discriminate between things). It also helps them retain and recall information, such as numbers, letters, words and figures.

Art activities like beadwork, origami, sculpting and pottery even help develop visual-spatial skills essential at school. Strong visual-spatial dexterity aids a child in subjects, such as science, technology, English (reading, writing and comprehension) and mathematics (especially geometry).

Fosters communication and language development: Art also helps children develop their vocabulary and language skills[14]. Art projects can help even preschoolers express themselves effectively by talking to each other about the activity while it's on. It is not only an opportunity for them to learn the names of colours, shapes and textures, it also helps them grasp some descriptive words during these hands-on activities. Words like 'cut', 'paint', 'paste', 'colour', 'red', 'dark', 'light', 'nice', 'round', 'sticky' are all used to discuss and explain their creations at hand. They even learn comparative words like bigger, smaller and sharper. As a parent, you can also contribute to their language skills by asking some basic questions about their artwork. You could ask them to describe their drawing when they show it to you, without of course making any judgements on their work.

Improves concentration: Creative art activities require focus because the child has to look at a painting and replicate it, colour or cut within edges, put a string through a bead, stick a fabric with glue, etc. All these activities require eye-hand coordination, which helps strengthen concentration and focus.

A child's massive urge to create needs to be valued by the parent. It is possible that they will end up learning a lot more when engaged in two-dimensional (origami, drawing, paper collage making) and three-dimensional (play dough, clay modelling, beadwork) art activities. So, make sure your child always has a good stock of art paper, crayons, water paints, plastic scissors, beads, beeswax/clay/play dough and pencils at home, along with a dedicated place to practise art. So, when you step into your little one's room, be ready to encounter a mishmash of colours on the walls, or the craft gear strewn on the floor like landmines! After all, it's all for a good cause!

SLEEP IS MASSAGE FOR THE MIND

As per the American Academy of Paediatrics[15], this is how much sleep children need:

- Toddlers (ages 1–2)   11–14 hours
- Preschoolers (ages 3–5)   10–13 hours
- Primary schoolers to pre-teens (ages 6–12)   9–12 hours
- Teenagers (ages 13–18)   8–10 hours

Adequate sleep for children has truckloads of benefits, such as expedited physical growth, resistance to diseases, energized body and mind, and weight control. But, we shall examine sleep in this section as one of the key facilitators of cognitive growth. Sleep plays a crucial role in rewiring and restoring the brain's functions. When the body is taking time out while sleeping, the brain is working diligently by assimilating all the information it received throughout the day, by stowing it away systematically. According to the research carried out at the University of Colorado at Boulder, the brain builds and strengthens connections between the left and right hemispheres of the cerebrum when we sleep. It is this symmetry and deep connection between the two hemispheres that is needed to strengthen memory, amplify creativity and enhance logical thinking. Studies show that Albert Einstein's genius has been attributed to the well-connected and symmetrical brain hemispheres. So, the ability of children to learn effectively can be deeply influenced by the quality and duration of their sleep.

Research says that thirty to sixty minutes of sleep during the day, after children return from school, is restorative and a habit worth fostering[16]. You can understand the worth of a good night's sleep once you know what sleep deprivation can do to a child's cognitive performance.

Effects of sleep deprivation:

- diminishes focus, leading to poor concentration
- affects memory adversely (especially long-term memory)
- impairs critical thinking and decision-making skills.

The impact of sleep deprivation on cognitive skills is likely to affect the academic performance of your child.

Sleep before midnight is much more effective than what follows thereafter. Every hour's sleep before midnight is equivalent to two hours of post-midnight sleep in qualitative terms. If you notice that your child is finding it hard to hit the sack at a decent time on a regular basis, it's time to take matters into your own hands. You need to sleep-train her strictly by winding down early every night and establishing a consistent bedtime schedule.

Tips to facilitate bedtime:

- Keep her off caffeinated drinks at least four to five hours before sleeping. It's not just tea and coffee that have caffeine. Even some aerated drinks have mild amounts of caffeine.
- Stop the use of all screens one to two hours before bedtime.
- Ensure that she doesn't exercise close to bedtime.
- Do not fix a TV in her bedroom.
- Dim household lights at least thirty minutes before her bedtime.
- A warm bath before lights out is a good sleep inducer.
- Read her a bedtime story.
- Ensure that she retires to bed at the same time every night.
- Try not to vary bedtime between weekdays and weekends too much.

Survey Takeaway: While most of the parents I interviewed, who have children between the ages of 6 and 12 years were satisfied with the eight to nine hours of shut-eye that their children were getting, 60 per cent of the parents of children between the ages of 13 and 18 years reported that their children's routines were a wee bit out of whack. Many of them did not go to sleep before midnight. Also, only about 40 per cent did some reading before going to sleep, while the rest were either engaged on their laptop screens or on social media via their phones before hitting the sack. Children exposed to these blue lights before bed, remained restless and awake for a while before they could fall asleep.

By making all the necessary changes in your child's bedtime routine to ensure a good night's sleep, you're not just safeguarding their waking hours from lethargy, but also preparing them to take on the next day with renewed zest!

EXERCISE IS AN INSTANT PICK-ME-UP FOR THE BRAIN

'All work and no play makes Jack a dull boy!'

It may have been a cliché since forever, but I've been one firm advocate of this maxim for a long while now. Especially because the 'play' enhances the quality of 'work' that Jack puts in at school.

There's just too much laid out on a child's plate these days. Their daily schedule is chock-a-block with one activity after another, and twenty-four hours seem a little too less in a day. Many children are pressured by their parents to shun outdoor play and fitness activities before and during exams to 'focus' on studies. Exercise, in fact, refreshes children and helps them unwind completely. And a child who is not stressed out is likely to not only focus more, but also enjoy life in general.

Here's why rough-and-tumble play is important for a child's cognitive growth:

- It helps children focus better and keeps restlessness under check.
- Exercise enhances children's reading, comprehension and maths proficiencies. There is mounting evidence that the brain grasps vocabulary and language expressions more rapidly after exercise.[17-19]
- Owing to the increased blood flow to the brain, exercise facilitates memory and, thus, increases retention and recall of information.
- Free play fires up the imagination, helping children to tap into their creativity.

Therefore, help your child in his cognitive growth by encouraging him to step out of the four walls of the house to play. His brain craves this rough-and-tumble fun!

LOVE MAKES THE BRAIN REBOUND

When a child is raised in a loving environment full of positivity and emotional support, it gives him a sense of security, which accelerates his capacity to learn. When a toddler is lovingly engaged by the parent through eye contact, touch, body language and verbal exchange with a rich vocabulary, the neural pathways and connections in his brain are strengthened and wired together. This 'wiring' reinforces learning of language, problem-solving and reasoning skills.

BOOT OUT DISTRACTIONS, SAY 'HELLO' TO ATTENTION

Sometimes, it's only a little debugging of your home environment rather than a rewiring of the brain that can get things rolling on the study table. Nixing distractions around your child's study time can actually increase concentration and focus. Distractions often lead to procrastination that can squander precious study time, resulting in inadequate understanding of major concepts of homework.

How to get the most out of study time:

Fix a time: This could be a time when your child has taken some refreshments and rest after coming home from school, or after returning from outdoor play in the evening.

Designate a frill-free study zone: The area should be very comfortable, with a generously sized work desk and a comfortable chair. Ideally, there shouldn't be too many adornments or works of art in the immediate visual zone of your child while she is studying. This helps to keep the child from getting distracted. Make sure that the area around the study table is very neat, stripped of all clutter and is equipped with just the essential gear needed for studies. Unadorned and functional surroundings in the visual scope are calming to the senses. Without the disarray of objects in her view, her attention and focus are bound to improve.

Make it a well-lit space: Adequate lighting is an absolute necessity for studies. It is worth investing in table lamps and wall lighting designed especially for comfortable reading purposes that lessens eye strain and fatigue, thereby leading to increased productivity.

Ensure silence or white noise, as the case may be: Noises or voices filtering into the study room from the rest of the house can be distracting, or may become a big lure for the child to start procrastinating and shun work. But, while silence helps most people to focus on the work at hand, some children prefer background sounds and bustle around them to be able to concentrate. If your child can study only in silence, minimize noise in her study space. If total silence is not a likelihood in your house because of regular guests, a small baby in the house or the house being in close proximity to a busy road, you could invest in a pair of noise-cancelling headphones that reduce the background noise effectively. And for those who 'need' some background noise to study, you could provide them with a playlist of classical, instrumental or any other light background score that could help them focus.

Put away screens during study hours: Let there be a study-time decree that there would be no screen time (other than computers used specifically for homework) until studies are done. Phones should be put on 'silent' mode or completely out of reach for those stipulated hours. 'Out of sight, out of mind' may actually be an effective way of cutting out gadget distraction during studies.

Survey Takeaway: Mothers like Prasana Ramakrishnan, Priyadarshini Rao, Gowri Ravi and some other parents followed the austere approach of cutting off the TV connection completely to weed out the lure of the big screen. Only 7 per cent of all the parents surveyed said that their children (out of which two are teenagers) haven't been given mobile phones at all.

Accept the computer as a study-buddy: A computer cannot be completely banished from children's study tables in today's scenario. There is just too much homework that needs to be done online or requires the assistance of the Internet, making it a necessary distraction. But if you're apprehensive that your child may be sneaking into social media or browsing the Internet surreptitiously, you need to monitor the Internet usage, for sure! You could check on a younger child periodically to make sure that she is making good use of the computer. It will also be useful to design the layout of the room in such a way that the computer screen faces the entrance of the study room. Since constant monitoring is sometimes seen as being intrusive and impractical by teens, you should consider setting up a blocking software that filters Internet use by blocking some websites, such as Google's Simple Blocker or Habyts' Study Time. It is best to instil self-discipline in your child by encouraging her to switch on this blocker for the duration of the study period. This will foster a feeling of trust in your child. You definitely don't want her to think you're playing a policing role in the house!

Sanction regular breaks: It can get wearisome for many children to study for long stretches of time, as their brains need a reboot now and then. Taking quick five–ten-minute-long breaks after every hour of study can rejuvenate children and help them refocus.

ROUTINE AND STRUCTURE UNSCRAMBLE THE BRAIN

We know it just too well that it is very easy to fritter away precious hours idling or being consumed by screen fixation. But alas! There are only so many hours in a day. The days tend to fly past in a flurry of distractions and, before you know it, it's exam time already! Before your child loses his nerve and pushes the panic button, get a grip on the situation. You need to put a structure and routine in place from the beginning of the academic term itself, so that he doesn't feel gutted by the massive mountain of pending projects and assignments.

Ways to weave structure into study time:

Make a daily timetable: Dedicate a few hours every day to homework and studies. Ensure that your child adheres to this regime as best as he can. This will help him set aside time for studies, regardless of whether he has any pending homework or not. You could consider fixing a whiteboard in your child's room to help prioritize assignments. Some children prefer sticky notes to writing on the board. Let them use whatever helps them to organize their homework well.

Fix an elaborate planner for older children: By the time children are in middle school, their home assignments and projects become more complicated and demanding, requiring much more detailed planning. At this stage, it is more pragmatic to simplify the workload and break it down on a full term, monthly, weekly and daily basis. This can make the workload much more manageable. Your child's full-term plan should cover term goals, all major assignments with dates and other academic mileposts. His weekly schedule should include assignments for the coming week which should be put together on the weekend of the current week. His daily schedule should include progress updates on the weekly schedule, preparation for the next day at school and homework to be completed for the day.

The best tool to achieve this is a wall calendar and an annual diary. Invest in a large calendar or three medium-sized calendars. Divide the big calendar into three sections for the term, the week and the days of the week. If you've bought three separate calendars, label each similarly for the term, the week and the days of the week. Help your child to jot down important assignments and mileposts with their due dates. Mark these assignments with different colours to help prioritize more urgent or important ones so that they can be completed on priority.

Once the wall calendar and diary have been filled in, help your child to carry out the daily, weekly and monthly reviews of what has been achieved so far and what needs to be done next. The daily review can be done every evening, the weekly review can be done on a Friday or a Saturday each week, and the monthly review can be carried out at the beginning of the last week of each month. This is a process that will help him all through his life, as it can be applied even in his work life, post student years.

Employ the time-blocking concept: One great time-management technique that can work in unison with the calendar is the time-blocking concept. Cal Newport has spoken about this concept in great detail in his book *Deep Work*. You can help your child prioritize assignments and divide the workload into manageable bits by blocking out time slots in the daily schedule according to subjects or assignments in their order of importance and urgency. For instance, the first sixty to ninety minutes, when the child is feeling fresh and charged up, can be allotted to preparing for an upcoming exam or a project to be submitted the next day; the next forty-five minutes can be assigned to another subject which doesn't need an equally sharp focus (since it's a law of diminishing returns for the energy levels after a point), and so on. These blocks of time should be uninterrupted with no distractions, except for pre-planned breaks after every forty-five minutes or one hour.

Encourage them to maintain a flip notepad in school: A small notepad that can be used to note down anything that the child needs to remember or track, and to create his to-do lists, is a handy tool. A lot of homework instructions are conveyed verbally by the teachers to the students which may sometimes be hard to recall once they're home. In such a scenario, flip notepads come in handy, to quickly scribble a few words about each verbal instruction from the teacher. It then becomes easy for the child to recall all the directives given by the teacher, exactly as they were conveyed. This to-do list can then be transferred onto the calendar into relevant sections.

Consider using a timer: You could use the 'timer' option on a mobile phone to help your child beat stress and fatigue. The timer can be set for a stipulated duration and the child is then expected to study wholeheartedly during the said period. When the timer goes off, the child gets to take a break. This cycle can be repeated a couple of times if it's a reasonably long study duration. The rounds of committed studying and breaks can refresh and revitalize the child if he finds it tedious to focus on studies for one prolonged stretch.

The Pomodoro Technique, invented by Francesco Cirillo when he was a university student, is a globally practised time-management approach that can be adopted by children for their studies. In this approach, a child can study for a period of twenty-five minutes followed by a break of five minutes. This thirty-minute slot is called a Pomodoro. The study time of a child can be broken up into as many Pomodoros as required, depending on how much time he needs for his studies. You can tweak this approach to match the specific requirements of your child.

Establishing a study-time routine to facilitate learning may take some time and a few iterations initially as it is a trial-and-error process. But once it is put in place, it can be very rewarding and worth all the effort.

UNSTRUCTURED PLAY KEEPS THE BRAIN FOG AWAY

Unstructured outdoor play stimulates the intellect in the following ways:

Enhances children's sense of wonder: Free play allows children to discover their surroundings which can heighten their sense of wonder. It sharpens their power of observation, imagination, sense of exploration and critical-thinking ability. When they play without structure, they learn new concepts, such as: why some things float while others sink when they put objects in a tub of water. They may learn about friction by running with and without socks, and so on.

Teaches vital science and maths concepts: Children can discover certain patterns and symmetry in trees, waves of the sea, flowers, snowflakes and wind ripples. The concepts of similarities and differences can be learnt by observing that while all species of fish differ from each other, they are similar in one respect, they all have fins. Children also get to learn sorting and classification when they sort and classify different types of leaves, barks, flowers, pebbles and shells based on their unique characteristics.

Teaches crucial life lessons: When children indulge in free play, they learn life lessons by using the five traditionally recognized methods of perception:

- **sense of taste** teaches them that mud should not be eaten, and that there are different types of tastes like sweet, sour, bitter and salty;
- **sense of touch** teaches them that thorns on bushes can prick and hurt and, therefore, they have to be avoided;
- **sense of smell** teaches them that flowers are fragrant, or a rotten apple smells bad and should not be eaten;
- **sense of sight** teaches them to appreciate differences in colours, birds, insects, animals, sizes, shapes and much more;
- **sense of hearing** teaches them to differentiate between various sounds like those of birds, insects, animals, etc.

4

Active Play

'Play is the highest form of research.'

ALBERT EINSTEIN

I REMEMBER WHEN I was young, I would play outdoors for two hours straight, and that, it was non-negotiable. My friends and I couldn't wait to get out of the house to play with the other children in the neighbourhood. My most precious childhood memories revolve around simple outdoor fun activities, like hopscotch, pitthu, hide-and-go-seek, and four corners. That was the daily dose of fun for all the children in our times!

When children run, jump, squat, throw a ball, ride a bicycle, skate, climb a hillock, they build muscle strength, learn to balance and their eye-hand coordination improves. The TV, laptop, gaming console, tablet and smartphone have become the primary 'play' for the majority of children today. It comes as no surprise that children today are aerobically much less fit than my generation was. Many parents today admit that their children are hooked on one gadget or the other, and that it has become a Herculean task to motivate them to leave the four walls of the house to go and play.

What is active play, you may wonder? 'Active play is physical activity with regular bursts of a moderate to vigorous pace, such as crawling, jumping, or running. Active play should raise children's heart rate and make them "huff and puff".'[20]

Active play is crucial for every child once they master the skill of walking.

Active play can occur in various ways:

- indoors or outdoors
- alone or with friends or family
- in structured settings, such as swimming lessons or other sporting activities
- in unstructured settings, such as backyards or parks.

There are many benefits of active play, such as:

Physical development

- It improves gross and fine motor skills.
- Activities like cycling, skating, jumping rope, climbing a tree, gymnastics, football and hula hoop enhance balance, eye-hand coordination, agility and flexibility.
- It helps maintain a healthy weight.
- It builds physical resilience by keeping children healthy and robust.
- It helps to strengthen muscles and build bone mass.
- It enhances the quality of sleep as a result of the energy expenditure.

Cognitive development

- It sharpens focus and attention, that further improves

reading, comprehension and maths skills.
- It boosts memory.

Emotional development

- It provides children with a sense of acceptance and belonging when they play with other children.
- It builds their self-esteem and fortifies self-confidence by giving them a sense of accomplishment with new friends.
- It helps children to strengthen their emotional resilience by learning to manage their emotions, especially in a group or a team-play situation.

Life skills

- Active play provides a great platform to build social skills, as children make friends, bond with them and trust each other. Your child may end up forming lifelong friendships while playing.
- It enhances language and communication skills.
- It teaches children character attributes such as patience, cooperation, sharing and fair play.
- It helps them build leadership qualities and hones their team skills.
- It helps them to become self-sufficient.
- It prepares children to be good losers, as it is unrealistic for one child to always win in a free play or a sport. They may win some and lose some. Active play teaches them to be a 'good sport'.

Survey Takeaway: Nimisha Warrier, the mother of a 13-year-old, says that she and her husband have often explained to their son that participation itself is a great step, and winning every time should not be the only goal. Losing doesn't mean that he is a failure. Working hard at whatever he does and giving it his best shot, is more important than just winning. And ever since, they've noticed a positive change in him. He now thoroughly enjoys playing, without the worry of losing or winning!

- It helps them build leadership qualities and hones their team skills.
- It helps them to become self-sufficient.

DIFFERENCES BETWEEN ACTIVE INDOOR AND ACTIVE OUTDOOR PLAY

Active indoor play: Younger children, who have just mastered the ability to walk and need close supervision, can benefit even from indoor play. For them, even the house is big enough to indulge in ample active play. Some games that encourage movement that you could play with your little one, are: running and catching; dragging empty cardboard boxes around; throwing or kicking a soft ball; making an obstacle course at home; dancing to favourite rhymes or songs; pillow fights; hide-and-go-seek; tricycle or toy vehicle rides. You can actually keep it all simple by using household items, such as a soft ball, rope, pillow, cardboard boxes and food cartons.

For older children, indoor active play can be in the form of fitness classes held in the studios, such as dance, aerobics, yoga and trampoline classes. These can benefit school-going children of all ages.

Active outdoor play: This form of play is highly recommended for children of all age groups. Children love open spaces, as these allow them the freedom to shout and laugh aloud, something otherwise forbidden! Besides, it gives them ample space to run around freely. Outdoor play is also more favoured for all the benefits that playing in the open spaces affords to children, as discussed in the earlier chapters.

It is our responsibility as parents to encourage our children to step out to experience a brighter and more positive world that lies right outside the four walls of our homes. We should help them build a habit of active outdoor play for an hour or two daily, for all the benefits it offers.

Active play is of two types: unstructured and structured.

Unstructured active play

Unstructured active play, as the name itself suggests, is completely spontaneous and self-motivated play. It isn't organized like structured sports. It is improvised as children make up their own play on the spot. It has no preordained rules or instructions, and is changeable according to the whims of the children participating in it. This type of play has no coaches, trainers, teachers or other adults to direct it and is purely children-led. Children make rules while on the go, and it is they themselves who regulate each other's conduct.

This is an open-ended play with no set time limits or specific strategy. Children tend to move at their own pace in free play. Unlike structured play, unstructured active play can be extended for hours if allowed. There are no organized teams here. It can be a solo play, a group play or can be a play with teams created on-the-spot by children. Playmates could be in the form of siblings, peers, or even parents (more in case of younger children). It does not require any specific equipment. Children can chase each other or climb a tree or play kho-kho without needing any playing gear. However, unstructured active play could require simple gear like a ball, skipping rope, hula hoop, bicycle, according to the preference of the players.

Unstructured active play is an enriching experience for children. They have a primal urge to move. They need to experience with movement, which can be in the form of running, climbing, rolling, skipping, jumping, etc. They eagerly explore and challenge their limits through impromptu play and, in turn, learn new things about what their bodies are capable of.

> 'Children's play flourishes when we "let it"
> rather than "make it" happen.'
>
> —KIM JOHN PAYNE, *SIMPLICITY PARENTING*

Survey Takeaway: Gowri Ravi has always known the benefits of unstructured play. She remembers her childhood as being a very happy and a stress-free one as she grew up playing outdoor games and board games with her friends regularly. She wanted to ensure that she provided an enriched childhood to both her daughters (currently 20 and 11 years old) too. Therefore, she made sure that their play time was never compromised at the cost of any other activity. She let them dabble with various physical activities and free play. She also taught them cycling and skating, so that they didn't always have to be dependent on friends, to be able to play.

Perks of unstructured active play

Enhances emotional well-being: Unstructured active play is a significant way of reducing the incidence of anxiety and depression[21-23] by helping children release stress through fun, laughter and interactions with each other.

Stimulates exploration and imagination: Children learn to make their own games with their own rules and strategies without the pressure of a serious goal in mind. It gives them the freedom to try out new things, fail sometimes, and then learn from their mistakes. Open-ended play leads them towards self-discovery through diverse experiences.

Hones decision-making skills: By working collaboratively, children work on conflict resolution and decision-making abilities. They even learn the negotiation skills that help them to think independently.

Helps them develop empathy: While playing with others, children learn to become sensitive towards others and respect their perspective as well.

Provides unbridled joy: Children associate unstructured active play with fun, freedom and rejuvenation that no structured sport can provide to them.

Ideas for unstructured active play

- free play in the park, playground or backyard with friends or siblings, active games like hide-and-go-seek, hopscotch, pitthu, kho-kho, four corners, etc;
- for preschoolers, it could be playing on a swing, merry-go-

round, jungle gym, hula hoop, playing with a ball;
- running/walking in a park, on a beach or through a nature trail;
- climbing a hillock;
- riding a bike in the neighbourhood lanes;
- climbing a tree;
- leisure swimming;
- leisure running;
- jumping rope;
- walking the dog;
- a day hike with family and/or friends.

A minimum of sixty minutes of unstructured active play every day is highly recommended for children to reap most of its benefits[24-25]. Resist the urge to meddle while your child plays with his friends. Give him a free hand in his play so that he can learn some crucial life skills, like independence in solving problems and decision-making. You just need to watch over him for his physical safety, and stay in his visual range, should he need you.

Structured Active Play

Structured active play is an organized physical fitness activity or a sport that is led by an adult, generally a fitness coach or a physical training instructor. There is a specific time, a fixed place and a set of rules for this kind of play. An adult leader is at the helm of the planning and execution of this activity. Structured play is generally directed by a goal, which is why it is also known as 'play with a purpose'. The goal may be winning, mastering an activity, being part of a popular sports team, gaining fitness, losing weight or simply to unwind. These activities could either be a part of the school curriculum or pursued as an after-school interest by joining a sports academy, fitness classes or by hiring a personal coach.

Structured active play can be either in the form of an organized sport or some physical activity classes.

Benefits of structured active play:

Helps build critical character traits: Structured active play affords children an opportunity to build character by helping them to acquire personal qualities, such as diligence, dedication, self-discipline and accountability. A child who plays a team sport will learn to demonstrate good sportsmanship. Children playing sports learn to be fair and to respect other players. They become more responsible towards their entire team by sharing responsibilities as well as credit, rather than just being self-absorbed in their own benefit.

Helps discover a passion: Children who are introduced to structured sports may discover their true calling while playing that sport, and may go on to excel in it.

Teaches vital life skills: Children learn essential life skills through organized sports, such as coping mechanism, resilience and individualism. Being associated with a sport can also give a child a deep sense of identity. All these competencies can be invaluable throughout a child's life.

Helps gain insights about other sports: Children who receive formal coaching in the sport of their interest, not only end up learning about their own sport, but also gain sufficient insights about many other sports. When a child is passionate about a sport, he is likely to be curious to learn about other sports too, because of the general love for sports.

Is a great stress buster: Although playing a sport sounds serious compared to unstructured play because it has structure, purpose, rules and adult supervision, to many children who are very passionate about their sport, a field with their favourite sport can be the best stress buster that helps them loosen up like no other activity can.

Confers a lifetime of fitness: When a child discovers his love for a sport and learns it well, he is very likely to 'play it till he is fit to play, and stays fit till he plays it'. And this may last him a lifetime, helping him to stay fit and healthy all through his life.

There are two kinds of structured active play:

Organized sports

- Children can either choose to play an individual sport or be part of a team sport.
- Some popular individual sports are swimming, gymnastics, tennis, badminton, track and field athletics, golf and archery.
- A few team sports which are popular with today's children are cricket, football, hockey and basketball.

Physical activity classes

This is yet another form of structured active play besides sports. It has most of the components of a structured sport. There is physical exertion, through moderate to vigorous movement. It is an organized activity which is mapped and drawn up before the start of the session and is led by an adult who is a fitness coach or a physical training instructor. There is a designated place for the activity (outdoor or indoor) with specified timings for different sessions. It has a structure to follow. For instance, a dance class may have three segments: warm-up, dance and cool down. Unlike unstructured active play which is purely for fun and stress relief, participants here may have different goals for joining the classes. The goals may be losing weight, learning a new skill, increasing energy levels through the day, becoming fitter, building confidence, making friends, lowering stress, and so on. Physical activity classes may either be a part of the school curriculum or pursued later in the day by attending a group fitness class or by hiring a personal coach.

The difference between sports and fitness classes lies in the fact that sports often (if not always) foster competition, while these fitness classes do not usually involve any competition. Examples of physical activity classes or one-on-one sessions are school PT, aerobics, dance, yoga, taekwondo, karate, roller skating, martial arts and strength training sessions at the gym (for older children). Such sessions can do a lot of good to the following type of children:

- those who are too lazy to step out for free play and their parents have to put in a structured activity to get them to exercise;
- those who are shy, self-conscious or have low self-esteem and fear rejection, ridicule and aggression by peers in a free play or a sports setting;
- those who are overweight and need extra exercise over and above free play.

Why unstructured active play is an absolute necessity for children

While both unstructured and structured active play have their place under the sun, sports or physical activity classes at the cost of active unstructured play can deprive a child of all the goodness and fun that free active play offers. It is really great to have your child learn a sport, but I implore you not to eliminate free active play from their daily routine. There is a lot at stake for your child when unstructured play is completely substituted by structured active play. The benefits of free play immensely outweigh the worth of organized sports and activities.

These days, the balance is tipped heavily in favour of structured and scheduled activities for our children. We may be adding these to our children's already tightly packed schedules, leaving them feeling overburdened. If you're a parent who is trying to give your child as many possibilities as you can, by way of exposure to a number of fitness and other extracurricular activities, you need to pull yourself back a bit and think twice! If you could enter your child's body and mind, and imagine life from their perspective, it's sure to leave you aghast at the amount of physical, mental and emotional stress they may be under. There is school to attend, homework to finish, extra-curricular activities to undertake, deadlines to meet, competitions to take part in, peer pressure to win these competitions, other parental and peer expectations…and the list goes on! There just seems to be very little or no time for family interactions or for free play. When these little souls are spread too thin, there can be a snapping point which may manifest itself in some form or the other. Children need free play to diffuse their daily stress and come back revitalized to take on the next day with renewed enthusiasm.

Active Play • 93

While the virtues of unstructured active play have been etched out in detail earlier in the chapter, here's the argument in favour of free play vis-a-vis organized sports and fitness activities in a nutshell.

Benefits of Free Play	Benefits of Organized Play
1. Spontaneous and self-motivated play. Hence, it helps children unwind and unleash their creativity and the spirit of discovery.	1. Structured and controlled by adults with a set of rules. There is rigidity which may be stressful for some. Very little scope for exploration and creativity. Not recommended for preschoolers.
2. No performance pressure. Freedom, laughter and friends make this play pure fun. So, low incidence of anxiety.	2. Can be highly competitive, with too much emphasis on winning. This can be physically demanding and emotionally draining, as every child who plays cannot win.
3. No equipment needed. Just a little space for rough-and-tumble play. The gear needed (if at all) is very basic. Not only economical, but doesn't even demand much of your involvement and time.	3. Coaching, gear and uniform could cost a fortune. Most coaching sessions require commutes and are therefore time consuming.
4. Works for all age groups. Helps younger children enhance their balance, flexibility and fine motor skills through movements like jumping, running, catching, kicking and skipping.	4. Many organized sports do not necessarily work on improving balance, flexibility and fine motor skills. Younger children struggle with rules and tight control.

So, step back and resist the urge to sign your child up for too many activities. Instead, declutter her schedule of too many adult-driven activities, and make sure that she gets a decent amount of time for unstructured free play. And if you find that your child's daily schedule is bursting at its seams with so many organized activities that she doesn't get time for free play, then it's a warning sign that you need to take certain things off her timetable at the earliest.

If you have to make a choice between an organized sport/a fitness activity and unstructured active play for your child, do not cut out free play completely from their day. This could take away a lot of joy from their lives. If a structured activity has to be added, figure out a balance between the two as best as you can without, of course, putting too much additional pressure on your child and impinging on their time.

Remember, you need to let your child explore the outdoors by experimenting with different fitness activities. Do not pressurize her to enrol for any of the structured activities in haste. Let her be the one to put a finger on the activity of her liking rather than you choosing it for her. This way, she is likely to enjoy the activity and sustain it for a long time. If a child is forced to sign up for a sport or fitness activity, she is likely to quit it sooner than you may imagine.

Remember, modern-day children are at an immense risk of spending their childhood in fierce pursuit of achievements at the cost of having unadulterated fun. So, give them back their childhood by allowing them the freedom to play freely and flourish!

'If we watch a young child at play, we can see that through her constant sensory/physical interaction with the environment, she gains experience and understanding of the situation, of herself, and the relationship between the two. She comes to know herself, the world, and what flows between.' Says Sharifa Oppenheimer in her book *Heaven on Earth: A Handbook for Parents of Young Children*.

5

Character-building

'Young bodies are like tender plants, which grow and become hardened to whatever shape you've trained them.'

DESIDERIUS ERASMUS, DUTCH HUMANIST

VALUES ARE THE foundation of a child's identity. They're like a lighthouse guiding the child through the voyage of life. Without providing a strong base made of strong moral values, we would be leaving our children in a rudderless boat to drift in any direction that the wind takes them, rather than helping them chalk out their own precise course and stay on it steadfastly. Sans a good value system in place, children would be left vulnerable to negative social influences, be it of the media, Internet or peers. These are potent enough to crush an 'unformed' person so ruthlessly that it would be a Herculean task to pull them out of this abyss. Instilling moral virtues at a young and impressionable age will not only protect your child from this onslaught, but will also give them an identity, individuality and a perspective strong enough to help them stand their ground during challenging situations.

Instilling these values is time-consuming, and many parents are crunched for time. The fallout? Outside influences, such as social media, TV and peer pressure fill in the gap left by parents. If we do not wish to be swamped with remorse for the rest of our lives for not giving a strong direction to our children, we need to consciously set aside time to teach these values to them. Teaching values begins at home. The earlier you start, the better it is for them.

Some essential moral values are:

- **Empathy and compassion:** Empathy is the heart of ethics, It embodies caring for others and being truly concerned about their welfare.
- **Honesty and integrity:** It is our ability to act in conformity with the ideals, beliefs and the morality we hold true, in all situations, however trying they may be. Speaking the truth and acting truthfully in our conduct, relationships and in our dealings with others is essential. Honesty is very closely linked to integrity in its essence.
- **Fairness:** Being impartial, unbiased and unprejudiced; not taking advantage of anyone, especially of a weaker person; and promptly acknowledging mistakes, are the markers of fairness.
- **Perseverance and diligence:** Working hard persistently, taking care of even the minor details in the process, shows perseverance and diligence.
- **Respect:** Honouring the worth of every person and treating them with dignity, regardless of who they are, what they do, and where they come from; being courteous, civil and considerate; respecting differences of all types, such as caste, colour and economic strata, these are the basic tenets of respect.

- **Gratitude:** Showing deep appreciation and thankfulness for what we have in our lives, rather than focusing on what we don't have.
- **Courage:** Having the ability to stand up against all odds and overcome obstacles rather than surrendering to them, and going all the way to finish what we start, is courage.
- **Ability to resist gratification:** It is resisting unhealthy temptations with the help of self-restraint and strength of character. It also represents the ability to withstand the lure of self-destructive habits, such as smoking, drugs, alcoholism and fixation on inappropriate content.
- **Individuality:** Cultivating a uniqueness of character that differentiates a person from others, is individuality.
- **Reliability:** Reliability is to possess the quality of honouring commitments, being consistent and trustworthy.
- **Responsibility:** Being accountable for what one does and for who we are. Being in control of one's choices and therefore, of one's life. The strength of character to neither shift blame when the going gets tough, nor claim credit for the work of others. Having these attributes is a sign of being responsible.
- **Humility:** Being modest is being humble. It is the feeling that your social standing does not make you superior to others.

Parents are the most influential teachers and the safest sources of these life virtues. So, how do you teach these values to your child? Here are some interesting and effective ways of instilling values in children:

TEACHING VALUES THROUGH CANDID DISCUSSIONS

We need to have planned 'value-inducing sessions' once in a while to help children understand the importance of learning moral values. The essence of each value, its importance in life, and the consequences of flouting it, need to be explained to children very explicitly. You should impart these valuable life lessons in age-appropriate language. It needs to be impressed upon them that if they act according to good values, good things will happen to them; but if they spurn these values and act in unworthy ways, bad tidings could fall upon them. Give them specific examples of good and bad behaviour. Talk unambiguously about the values you uphold, and why they are so important to you. The earlier you start, the better are the chances of them having a good start and a strong foundation of positive values. Continue these conversations throughout their adolescence and teen years. Make these discussions regular and age appropriate. Your regular conversations will help your child impose trust in your ability to help them deal with moral dilemmas in the future too.

The children of parents who do not converse with them often, may reach out to peers for advice in times of moral quandary. To avoid this, ensure that your child has a solid support system, be it in the family or outside home. Take a relative or a teacher into confidence. You want to avoid any negative influences on the child's life, even if it's a friend or a family member.

'If you don't address these issues with your kids, society will fill in the void,' says Gary Hill, Ph.D., director of clinical services at The Family Institute at Northwestern University.

For instance, in order to keep your child off substance abuse, talk vividly about the dangers of indulging in these activities. Talk about the dangerous health consequences and the legal repercussions of doing drugs. Talk about the fact that drugs lead to addiction, can derail a person and ruin their life. Such a detailed face-to-face discussion will allow children to make smart choices as teens and later as adults.

DISCUSSING VALUES THROUGH 'TEACHABLE MOMENTS'

With many children, 'turkey talk' may not be a very effective way of imbibing moral values in them; more so, if you think that you lack the art of making a heavy topic like this sound interesting. Since talking about moral values is a life-impacting discussion, you need to ensure that you don't make these conversations into one-sided boring lectures, or else, you may lose those receptive little ears to sleep. This is one instance when discussing values through 'teachable moments' can come to your rescue. Teachable moments are the day-to-day incidents that can offer us an opportunity to teach our children about crucial values. Teachable moments are more effective than direct and upfront discussions, as these are based on real incidents and can be used as conversation starters. These could be incidents you and your child may witness in real life, read about in the news or watch in a film. You could talk about an incident that reflects an act of bravery by an individual who may be known to you. This could be a family member, a friend, an acquaintance or even be you! It could also be an incident that you would have read about in the news. Share it with your child and ask him what he thinks about the same. For instance, I came across a news article in 2013 about a 12-year-old daughter of a daily-wage labourer who showed exemplary courage by saving five children from drowning. Totally awestruck, I discussed this incident with my son (16 years old then) like I usually would. I asked him questions like: 'What do you think of the girl who saved those lives?' 'What would you have done if you were in the place of the girl?' I strongly think such incidents are good conversation starters that can teach our children virtues like courage, bravery and heroism.

To take another example, you and your child may be walking on the road and may witness a dog walker tugging very hard at a dog's leash, causing it great discomfort. While you and your child may be overcome with pity for the animal, it's an ideal conversation starter to discuss the importance of values, like showing compassion towards animals.

Keeping the lines of communication always open is one great way of ensuring that kids know that you're invested in their welfare. And that, they can trust you to help them if and when they find themselves stuck in a tight corner on their journey to adulthood.

ROLE MODEL: DO AS YOU SAY TO LEAD THE WAY

If you want your child to imbibe virtues, you need to lead by example. For instance, if you want your child to display honesty, you have to be sure to never lie in her presence. So, if she overhears you lying to your boss on the phone that you're sick and need the day off, when actually you're absolutely hale and hearty and need the day off for other not-so-serious reasons, you're giving your child conflicting signals. She may come to believe that lying is acceptable under certain circumstances.

Remember, however well you may teach a good value to your child verbally, it'll all be undone if your child senses incongruity between what you teach and what you practise.

LOVE AND QUALITY TIME ARE THE BEST ARMOURS AGAINST NEGATIVE SOCIAL INFLUENCES

Reports from the office of the National Drug Control Strategy, USA, show that strong family bonds can prevent children from developing drug problems. Showering children with love and investing time in their lives can help build their self-esteem. And children with high self-esteem and strong relationships at home are more likely to form their character based on the moral values they learn from their parents. Their sense of self-worth and emotional fulfilment act as a strong filter for the outside world, that includes their selection of friends and the strong negative influences around them. The loving connection that you build with your child provides him with a strong sense of security, well-being and a mental resolve to resist these compelling negative influences in his life.

Various studies all around the globe point towards a potent connection between low self-esteem, drug addiction and alcoholism. Most teenagers who are victims of substance abuse or alcoholism are found to suffer from low self-esteem because of the lack of love and strong positive influences at home[26-29]. When children are not provided with a loving relationship, a sturdy moral fibre and sound guidance at home, they're likely to feel a sense of emptiness that makes them very vulnerable to the outside influences.

So, it is really worth being involved in our child's day-to-day life, and being aware of:

- how his day goes;
- what games he plays;
- who his friends are;
- how he is performing at school;
- any sudden mood changes;
- any withdrawn behaviour;
- what his interests are;
- how his general behaviour is towards peers and others;
- what concerns him.

Talk to him often to find out if there's something bothering him at school or in his various relationships. He should know that even in his most critical times, when he finds himself vulnerable to unhealthy influences, he can trust you completely to share his plight and fears, and that, you will be patient and will guide him with love and care.

INSPIRATIONAL BOOKS AND FILMS

Books and films with strong moral messages can help steer a child's sense of values in the right direction. Storybooks can help a child get inside a character's mind, feel their moral dilemma and watch them finally choose right over wrong. This can greatly influence a child's value system. Here are some examples of books that teach good values through stories:

- *Panchatantra* by Vishnu Sharma
- *The Giving Tree* by Shel Silverstein
- *The Invisible Boy* by Trudy Ludwig

- *The Bird with Golden Wings* by Sudha Murty
- *Rules* by Cynthia Lord
- *I Know Why The Caged Bird Sings* by Maya Angelou (for young adults)
- *The Story of my Experiments with Truth* by Mahatma Gandhi

'The right book can stir a child's empathy better than any lesson or lecture ever could, and the right book matched with the right child can be the gateway to opening his heart to humanity,' writes Michele Borba, clinical psychiatrist and author, in her book *UnSelfie: Why Empathetic Kids Succeed in Our All-About-Me World*.

Some films that we enjoyed as a family for their important life lessons are:

- *Do Ankhen Barah Haath*
- *Forrest Gump*
- *Bhaag Milkha Bhaag*
- *Mary Poppins*
- *Poorna*
- *I Am Kalam*
- *The Pursuit of Happyness*
- *The Lion King*

These films can greatly influence children to explore values, such as empathy, honesty, perseverance, integrity, courage and respect.

KNOW YOUR CHILD'S FRIENDS

There is a whole lot of truth in what Aesop (the famous Greek storyteller) once said: 'A man is known by the company he keeps.' Friends are one of the main influences in a child's life, especially after they enter adolescence. In fact, teenage is a stage in life when the influence of friends is much greater than that of parents. To ensure that your child doesn't get into bad habits through bad company, it's imperative for you to know who your child is hanging out with, where she goes with her friends and how they spend their time together. Knowing her circle of friends will help you keep her off undesirable activities.

In order to avert heartache and anxiety related to issues like the questionable character of your teen's friend, suspicion about how they may be spending their time together and whether they're involved in some detrimental activities, you have to take a few necessary steps. These are:

Know the basic information about your child's friends: You need to know their names, where they live, whether they're in the same school and grade as your child, and whether these friends have had any major disciplinary issues in school or otherwise.

Get to know them personally: Connect with them, invite them home and talk to them to know them better.

Find out a little about their parents: It is important for you to know about the kind of families these children come from: whether they're a close-knit family, whether they share simple common interests with your child and whether their family values are generally aligned with your own. This information is especially important if your child spends a lot of time with these friends or plans to visit their homes.

Talk to your child if you sense something is amiss: Never hesitate to talk to your child if you notice her friend acting strange around you, or if you're suspicious about the character or activities of your child's friend. By talking to your child about it, you may not only be preventing her from getting into undesirable activities, but may also be able to help her friend navigate through a serious moral crisis.

ALLOW MEDIA USAGE IN RESTRICTED DOSES

As discussed in a previous chapter, the media is another big influence on a child's belief system. It could be in any of the various forms, such as TV, social media, the Internet or music. While it may be next to impossible to detoxify your child completely from the screens (and it's not all bad too), it definitely is in your purview to limit their daily usage.

TV: As reiterated in an earlier chapter of this book, you can restrict the time and type of TV that your child chooses to watch. Studies have shown that regular exposure to TV shows that depict violence, rape and abusive language, are known to increase aggressive behaviour, especially in boys[30]. Many contemporary TV shows also idealize acquisitiveness, racism, indolence, flippancy, instant gratification and other such negative values. Even most music videos are sexually very explicit, and many lyrics overtly talk about sex, violence and drugs. These attributes are completely antithetical to the values we want to instil in our children.

Social media: Facebook and WhatsApp addiction can deeply influence a child's character and personality. Narcissism is one big negative offshoot of social media overindulgence. Posting pouting selfies and Photoshopped pictures every so often has become a favourite pastime with Facebook-, Instagram- and WhatsApp-obsessed youth. This is making many children very vain, self-absorbed and indolent.

The Internet: While Internet browsing has hordes of benefits for children, it can be a matter of serious concern too. It has the potential of exposing children to pornographic material accidentally or by design. The Internet can even introduce children to online gambling and plagiarism in academic work, and has the scope of spreading hatred between different religious groups.

In view of the compelling negative influence of various forms of media on children, the parents' role as their primary guardians becomes ever more critical.

Parents can put a check on unrestrained use of media through the following measures:

- installing parental controls to block access to hazardous sites, such as those related to pornography, extreme violence, cruelty and perversion;
- setting limits on the time spent on media;
- installing the TV and computer in a room easily accessible to parents with the screen facing the entrance;
- restricting the usage of mobile phones for younger children, and encouraging adolescent children to share their phone password with parents;
- educating and guiding your child from time to time about the dangers and pitfalls of excessive media indulgence and browsing age-inappropriate sites.

OFFER OPPORTUNITIES TO PRACTISE VALUES

As mentioned before, actions speak louder than words. When your child witnesses you practising the values that you preach, he is likely to learn more quickly than through a long preachy lecture. Taking this wisdom a notch higher, offer your child opportunities to practise these values in real life, which will help him build a really strong moral fabric. Here are a few suggestions that could help you achieve this:

Volunteering for community service work: Encourage your child to volunteer for community service work, through which he could help the underprivileged sections of the society.

Working for differently abled individuals: Give her an opportunity to work for organizations that take care of differently abled children. There are enough organizations worldwide that support autism, visually impaired kids and many other differently abled individuals.

Helping victims of natural disaster: Contribute your time and other material resources as a family to victims of natural disasters, such as floods, earthquakes and famines.

Working for animal welfare: Teach your child to be kind to animals and birds by visiting an animal rescue home with your child, securing help for an injured animal or bird, and so on.

Survey Takeaway: Priyadarshini Rao is an ardent animal lover and it doesn't come as a surprise that Maya (her 14-year-old daughter) loves animals deeply. Priyadarshini says, 'I encouraged Maya to feed stray dogs and cats from a very young age. During her summer holidays, she would pack kibble and make her rounds, looking for hungry strays. On many birthdays, she has spent her gift cash buying food for dogs and cats at the animal shelters. She even spends time there helping out with cleaning and de-ticking the animals.'

Volunteering for a favourite cause: Encourage your child to think of any cause that she relates most to, find an organization locally that supports that cause, and let your child volunteer her time regularly. It could be to teach poor children, spend time at old-age homes and orphanages, or any other cause.

Inculcating a habit of giving: Foster the habit of 'giving' in your child on a regular basis by asking her to hand out toys, stationery items, books, clothes or any other resources needed by your support staff. She could either give away things (in good condition) from her collection from time to time, or buy them out of her savings.

Survey Takeaway: A gritty single mom, Smita Gaidhani used to take her son (now 20 years old) to orphanages and camps for children with special needs, where they would spend time with the children, educating them or contributing other resources. By the time he was 10, he had relinquished fire crackers, something he loved, just to buy books and goodies for the children with his own savings.

Sponsoring a child's education: Consider sponsoring one of your support staff's child's education. Make sure you and your child meet the child you're sponsoring. This will sensitize your child towards the needs of others and strengthen the feeling of empathy.

Supporting people who're being discriminated against: Moral values, such as empathy or acceptance of difference can also be made part of your child's day-to-day life. For instance, if there is someone you know who feels discriminated against for any reason, such as class, caste or sexual orientation, you could ask your child what they feel about it, and how you along with your child, could extend support to the person.

When you initiate your child into the habit of 'giving' her time or other resources (however small) to people who need them, she is not only learning to be generous, but is also learning other vital virtues, such as compassion, respecting differences and feeling gratitude for what she has already been bestowed in her life with.

SET BOUNDARIES THROUGH DISCIPLINE

The word 'discipline' typically conjures up images of a stern parent, lambasting and whacking the child alternately in wild frenzy. However comical and exaggerated the image may be, this authoritarian parenting style exists indeed. Authoritarian parents are very strict, demanding and are control freaks. They have negligible tolerance for disobedience, and believe in strong punishments if rules are flouted. The children of these parents are generally timid, with low self-esteem. Now, that's one end of the disciplining spectrum. At the other end of the spectrum lies the uninvolved parent who is generally disinterested in what their child does. This 'checked out' parent expects nothing from the child, simply doesn't know how to handle misbehaviour, gives total freedom and gives disciplining a total miss. Both these extreme styles of parenting are damaging to the mental, emotional and social health of a child.

Then there is the permissive parent who, although very warm, is also very lenient. This parent hates confrontation and is more of a 'best friend' than a parent. This 'best friend parent' is too eager to maintain their 'friend' status and in the process, never wants to disappoint the child. This could go to the extent that not many clear-cut rules are set in the house. This parent could be staying up late in the night with the 'child friend' and watching a film together; blindly trusting the child's ability to stay safe by letting the adolescent hang out late with her friends; encouraging her to lie about her age and letting her open a Facebook account before she turns 13; letting the child snigger and make fun of an adult who dresses differently; and letting her get away being mean to her 'not so cool' classmate. In short, there are no consequences of breaking rules, as there are no rules to break. This parent has a hard time dealing with conflict and saying a definitive 'no'. They make their child's life so comfortable and privileged that the moment the child is asked to do something that she doesn't like, the child may get upset or throw a tantrum. Remember, younger children really need us as parents and not as friends, as they already have friends of their age. Someone has to be there to guide and discipline them whenever there's a need. The absence of that person can lead to disobedience, anarchy and, in worst cases, an awful showdown when liberty is stretched too far. They will have many friends in life, but you are the only parents that they will ever have! So, play that role responsibly.

Remember, a lack of total discipline can be a harbinger of serious issues in your child's life. And of course, over-leniency and complying with all your child's wishes (reasonable and unreasonable), are not the best ways to show love. You and your child both need to know that being strict is not the same as being mean. If she never hears you say 'no' to her, she may never be able to handle a 'no' from the world. She may grow up with a total disregard for rules, guidelines and acceptable values. She may have difficulty in coping with challenges outside the protection of home. Also, the message that you're giving her is that all kind of behaviour (including misconduct) is acceptable. What kind of a person will she grow up to be? She may turn out to be a person with little or no regard for authority, a person lacking empathy for those in need, irresponsible, and contemptuous of values like integrity and humility. You can see how big a disservice you would be doing to her by letting her get away regularly by defying rules. This will only leave her ill-prepared to face her future.

In our role as caring parents, we have to prepare our children for life, so that they're hardy enough to handle the challenges that life throws at them along the way. We are there to teach our children about good and bad behaviour, and the outcome of bad conduct. We are there to guide them and get them back on track when they lose their ability to judge a situation and make mistakes. And we are there to keep them safe by protecting them from harmful situations. All this is not possible when the line separating a parent from a friend is blurred. A certain amount of discipline is absolutely necessary. Parents need to be parents, not friends, at least till a certain age. We are duty-bound to have clearly spelled out rules in the house, to set limits and boundaries, and have expectations for admissible conduct from our children.

The most ideal parent is the authoritative parent, who strikes a balance between being authoritative and responsive.

This parent believes in exercising the right amount of control while being warm and communicative at the same time. They respect their child's opinion, yet are assertive when the child needs disciplining. As much as it corrects misbehaviour, the right amount of discipline helps children in almost every sphere of life.

To put the benefits down into simple words, discipline teaches children:

- to discern right from wrong;
- the importance of following rules and respecting boundaries;
- to have a strong character with essential values, such as empathy, compassion, respect, righteousness, humility, accountability and gratitude;
- to be resilient enough to be able to handle various challenges in life;
- to feel gratitude for what they have, and not to feel entitled, taking all the good things in life for granted;
- to postpone gratification and resist unhealthy temptations;
- to manage their emotions judiciously.

SOME GUIDELINES TO DISCIPLINE YOUR CHILD

Set rules of conduct for your children: These should include rules about no smoking, no drugs—not even a 'I just need to try it once to know what the hullabaloo is about', curfew timings, conversational boundaries, promiscuity (relevant to older kids) and everything else that concerns their welfare. Explain in no uncertain terms to the child that he won't always get what he wants, and cannot always have his way.

Explain the consequences of flouting rules: Spell out the rules and the consequences of violating these to your child very clearly and in an age-appropriate way. Clarify the rationale behind placing these limits, and how these are linked to your values that you want the children to follow. You can even quote incidents that are reported in newspapers and magazines where children faced severe consequences for violating such rules.

Penalize them when rules are disobeyed: Enforce the rules and penalize your child when boundaries are breached. Do not succumb to your instinct to ignore misconduct. Stand firm every time, so as not to confuse the child. Depending on the severity of the misconduct, it is okay to discipline them by grounding them, taking 'time out' and taking away some privileges. However, never use punitive measures to discipline them. Hitting them can traumatize them for life.

Survey Takeaway: Kanika Kush uses a very unconventional method to discipline her 8-year-old son when he is in a defiant frame of mind. She uses a backward counting approach that has been explained to him in no uncertain terms. So, if she starts counting backwards from 5, it means that her temper is just beginning to rise, he'd better watch out! 4 means a warning for him but gives him time to pull himself up, 3 means that she's really getting angry, 2 means he's asking for trouble, 1 means that she's on the brink and 0 is blowing the top. 0 is seldom reached. The situation is generally resolved between 2 and 1.

As Dr T. Berry Brazelton writes, 'A child needs limits and nurturance; neither one alone is sufficient for a child to grow.'

LET CHILDREN BE ACCOUNTABLE FOR THEIR ACTIONS

Accountability, or owning up responsibility for one's actions, is a precious virtue that parents must teach their children. Being responsible for one's actions is such a versatile attribute that it instinctively adds other virtues, such as integrity, diligence, perseverance, independence and humility to that individual's character.

Most children hesitate to own up to their small and big mistakes because of the fear of a severe reprimand or other harsh reactions from their parents that they may have experienced sometime in the past, on having confessed to some goof-ups. So, how do you help your children learn to take responsibility for their actions?

We can make our children accountable for their actions when we encourage them to own up to their mistakes, and neither react too harshly immediately, nor rush to shield them from the unpleasant consequences of their actions. It is important for them to understand that whenever they stand up to their mistakes and confess about them on their own, you will treat them patiently and sensitively. They should also know that bad actions will generally lead to undesirable repercussions. You should be there to support your child and help him come up with a solution to the problem, to quell his fears and to encourage him to take the bull by the horns. Step aside from this point onwards to enable him to face the consequences head-on, so that he grows up to be a responsible adult who can handle his problems independently.

Given below are two scenarios that involve two irresponsible children. Think of how you would react to these situations, and whether the suggestions given below are in consonance with your thinking.

1. **Your daughter breaks her friend's doll and doesn't own up:** She blames another child for having done the damage. You investigate and find out that all fingers point at your child. It is best that you advise your child to go and own up to her mistake, apologize to her friend, offer to get the doll fixed, and if the doll is beyond repair, offer to replace the doll.

2. **Your son has a school project that he's been procrastinating about:** He's been putting off this tough project for a week, and now it's time to submit it the next morning. Your son says that he sat on it because it was tough and boring. But, he cannot finish it now. He asks you to complete it for him, otherwise he skips school the next day to avoid a dressing-down from the teacher. Would you chip in to finish his homework on his behalf? I would recommend that while you may give constructive suggestions, let him attempt to write it himself. And in case he cannot finish it, let him know that he has to face the teacher, apologize to her and be ready for the punishment. This approach will help him become more responsible for his work in future.

Do not overreact or reproach your child sharply the moment she commits a mistake. It can trigger a 'fight' or 'flight' response in a child. Take a deep breath before responding. You can let the situation sink in slowly and let some time pass. You have to be very sensible and thoughtful in how you react, as your reaction will set the stage for how the child will handle a similar situation in the future. And, please skip the big moral lecture at this juncture. Listen to her side of the story patiently. If you find out that she has committed the mistake, explain to her that everyone makes mistakes and it's okay to slip up sometimes and learn from the situation. However, explain that it's not okay to lie. It is very important to be honest and tell the truth. Then, talk about what she could have done instead, and should do next time to avoid a similar situation. Also, let her know subtly that she is loved, whatever she may have done. If your child comes to you the next time and owns up to a blunder she committed, don't forget to praise her for being honest, and then help her weather the storm.

6

Nutrition

'You gotta nourish to flourish.'

UNKNOWN

A HEALTHY DIET is of paramount importance to the overall growth of a child. The significance of a balanced daily diet in a child's physical, cognitive and mental development cannot be undermined.

In a world where burgers, pizzas, French fries, cookies, doughnuts, sodas and chips are the undisputed kings, it's an arduous task to keep your child away from these banefully unhealthy fast foods forever. To add to the woes, the aggressive marketing undertaken by the food and beverage industry, with its enticing food visuals, isn't doing much good to the willpower of this junk-food-loving generation. The lure is irresistible, and the parents' bandwidth and resolve are insufficient to fight the junk food monster. So, they surrender to the will of their little and not so little brats for the sake of peace in the house. But, at what cost? The dire consequences take the form of obesity, type II diabetes, stomach ulcers, impaired digestion, and the list goes on! Parents have to take the reins of their children's diet into their hands, since it is too steep a price to pay to have their children falling prey to various lifestyle diseases.

By the time you finish reading this chapter, you'll be ready to spruce up your child's daily diet with all the information and hacks in your diet arsenal. The pay-off? A child with a healthy weight, strong bones and teeth, an efficient digestive system, a robust immune system and a rocking metabolism!

For a more detailed analysis of children's diet, you can read my book, *Parenting in the Age of McDonald's*.

A BALANCED DIET: SIMPLIFIED

A balanced diet is one that provides all the essential nutrients that young bodies need, to grow optimally. It is a good mix of macronutrients (lean proteins, complex carbohydrates and good fats) and micronutrients (vitamins and minerals) consumed on a daily basis. Add hydration (water) to the list to optimize the nutrient balance, and that's all is needed for the healthy physical and mental growth of a child. The recommended daily amount of each of the food groups greatly depends on the child's age, activity levels and appetite.

The following food groups form the bedrock of a balanced diet that children need all through the growing years for optimal growth and maintenance:

Vegetables of different colours: These are the powerhouses of vitamins and minerals. These should be part of at least two meals in a day. Include a variety of vegetables of different colours. Each colour contains disease-fighting compounds called phytochemicals. Here's the classification according to colours:

- dark green and leafy: spinach, broccoli, mustard greens, beet greens, green beans, cabbage, bok choy, peas, cucumber and capsicum
- red and orange: tomato, carrot, pumpkin, red bell peppers and sweet potatoes
- purple: beetroot, purple cabbage and eggplant
- white: cauliflower, mushrooms, garlic and onion
- brown: potato and ginger

Fresh fruits: Fruits are packed with disease-fighting micronutrients like vitamins A, B and C, iron, folate, potassium and calcium. These make a great choice of snacks for children, rather than the empty calorie junk food. Some fruits are very high in their nutrient profile, such as bananas, all types of berries, cherries, jamuns, grapes, watermelons, apples, plums, pears, lemons, pineapples, mangoes, oranges, peaches and kiwis. It is ideal to consume fruits in the form of fresh fruit and dried fruit rather than as juices. Juices are very high in simple sugars and lack essential fibre that a whole fruit provides. If juices are sometimes unavoidable, opt for fresh or cold pressed juices (without added sugar), rather than canned ones.

Whole grains: Children are generally very active, as they engage in free play and sports. They need complex carbohydrates in the form of whole grains to keep them fuelled through the day. Carbohydrates are also crucial for the central nervous system, brain, kidneys, muscles and for the heart to function in top gear. Whole grains are brimming with vitamins and minerals, such as iron, magnesium, selenium and fibre. Some worthy whole grain choices are oatmeal, amaranth (rajgira), sorghum (jowar), finger millet (ragi), whole grain corn, pearl millet (bajra), bulgur (cracked wheat), whole wheat with bran, buckwheat (kuttu), barley (jau), whole grain rye, brown and wild rice, and quinoa.

However, avoid refined or processed grains that come without the all-essential fibre. Simple carbohydrates that need to be snubbed are white bread, white pasta, white rice, refined wheat flour and its products, and breakfast cereals, such as fruit loops, chocolate or honey-based flakes/loops, sugary cornflakes, frosted flakes, chocolate or honey-coated puffed rice.

Legumes and lentils: These are rich sources of fibre and protein. They comprise dried beans like chickpeas, kidney beans, black beans, black-eyed beans, black chickpeas and soybeans; dals; dried peas and sprouts. Because these are quite high in fibre, they control blood sugar spikes and end up curbing unhealthy food cravings. One caveat while consuming foods from this group is that, never eat them raw, as they can be toxic in their raw form. Always soak them, and then, either boil them, sprout them or ferment them.

Lean meat, fish and poultry: Proteins are the building blocks of bones, muscles, tissues, cartilage, skin and blood in a child's body. Children need relatively large amounts of protein every day, for their physical and cognitive growth, and to repair bodily wear and tear. Meat, seafood, fish, poultry and eggs, besides dairy products, provide children with proteins. These foods are also excellent sources of vitamins and minerals like B12, iron and omega-3 fatty acids that aid growth. Dried beans, dairy products, lentils and legumes, nuts and seeds are the vegetarian sources of essential protein. Be wary of animal products high in saturated fats, such as processed meats like sausages, salami and fried meat.

Nuts and seeds: These are fine sources of good fats and protein.

Fats help the absorption of certain vitamins by our body. These give sustained energy, keep the heart healthy, provide cushioning for the vital organs, play a crucial role in brain development and are good for the skin, amongst other things. Nuts like almonds, walnuts, pistachios, cashews and peanuts, and seeds of flax, sesame, sunflower, chia and pumpkin are good sources of fats.

Low-fat dairy: Milk and dairy products like ghee, yogurt, paneer and cheese are packed with protein, calcium, potassium and magnesium, which are especially essential for bone health. Unless your child is underweight, choose low-fat dairy to avoid too much saturated fat.

Our dietary efforts are an investment in the proper and timely overall development of our children. I do know that it's a tough task in the current scenario, with junk food luring your little ones from every direction, playing havoc on their willpower to resist. Nevertheless, it's an effort worth putting in all the resolve you've got. The best time to start is when they're very young, as it only gets trickier to convince an adolescent or a teenager to change the way they eat. Their habits may have been formed and firmed up by then. With small and consistent changes in your child's everyday diet (and the diet of your entire family), you definitely can set the tone for a lifetime of healthy eating.

Survey Takeaway: Rupinder Anand is a mother of two girls (aged 13 and 9). In the initial years, both her daughters were fussy eaters and mealtimes were nothing short of a battleground for her. The mere sight of most vegetables triggered a tantrum. And trying to force-feed didn't make things easier. After a few years of daily confrontations at the table, she finally stumbled upon a solution that worked. She came up with little games and stories to make mealtimes fun and stress-free. She started giving funny names to dishes; told her daughters stories about their favourite toons and heroes eating these foods to get stronger; used vibrant coloured crockery and played a colour game wherein the girls had to choose three colours for their vegetables and fruits that they had to eat daily. And it all worked! Rupinder says, 'Now my girls eat pretty much everything...carrot, capsicum, spinach. They enjoy most of these, as they have learnt to appreciate different tastes.'

WATER: THE FINEST BEVERAGE TO LEVERAGE

Whenever there is any talk about a healthy and balanced diet, most of us end up having a discussion on the macros and the micros. We (including most Internet resources) seldom mention water, the lifeblood of our well-being, as a critical part of a regular diet. Often taken for granted, we need to monitor water intake even more in the case of children. They have smaller bodies and smaller stores of water, but carry out a lot more physical activity than adults. Children's bodies are also a lot less heat-tolerant than adults, and thus, they're more susceptible to getting dehydrated. Even cognitive performance drops substantially during hypohydration, when there is uncompensated loss of body water.[31]

Benefits of water:

Transports nutrients: Water helps to transport many nutrients to the blood and other internal organs.

Maximizes performance: Hydrating well before and during exercise maximizes physical performance. Even if one loses as little as 2 per cent of the body's water weight, it can have a dehydrating effect, leading to impaired performance. Water keeps the body cool by maintaining the body's internal water balance and regulating body temperature.

Improves cognitive ability: Adequate hydration has been proven to recharge a child's cognitive abilities. Even mild dehydration can negatively alter concentration, memory and the overall mental performance of a child.

Keeps the body healthy: A sufficiently hydrated body has a higher resistance to breakdowns. Dehydration can rob children of energy, cause headaches and illnesses like urinary tract infection and constipation.

Flushes toxins: Water helps the kidneys to flush out toxins and metabolic waste from the body. This toxin build-up can cause health concerns if left in the body for long.

Reduces bloating: Contradictory as it may sound, an adequate intake of water stops the body from retaining water. And water retention is one of the chief reasons for bloating. Hence, regular hydration helps maintain a healthy weight.

Reduces unhealthy bingeing: Drinking water regularly before thirst sets in, can prevent unhealthy food cravings. Enough water in the stomach sends a message to the brain that it is full and not hungry.

Symptoms and complications of dehydration

Dehydration shouldn't be taken lightly, like a casual headache. It can play havoc with the body if not addressed in time. With mild dehydration, a child can be a little sluggish and fatigued, which may even go unnoticed. But in severe cases, dehydration can be life-threatening.

Signs that a child may be dehydrated:

A dry mouth, tearless crying, fatigue, headache, light-headedness or dizziness, sunken eyes, irritability, constipation, muscle weakness, drowsiness, exhaustion, decreased/no urine output or dark yellow and smelly urine, listlessness, diminished concentration and difficulty thinking clearly are the signs of dehydration.

If not attended to in time, dehydration could lead to serious health complications, like heat cramps, seizures, cerebral edema, low blood volume shock, life-threatening heatstroke and kidney failure.

How much water is enough?

The amount of water or other water-based fluids that a child needs depends on many factors, such as age, gender, metabolism, physical activity level, environment and weather. However, there is a minimum recommendation of drinking water for kids as is for adults.

The approximate recommended daily amount of water is:

- 5–8 years: five glasses (1 litre)
- 9–12 years: seven glasses (1.5 litres)
- 13 years and above: eight to ten glasses (2 litres)

Children need to drink even more water in hot and sultry

weather, and before, during and after any strenuous physical activity.

Most parents surveyed were unaware of the serious repercussions of dehydration and hence, did not push or monitor their children's water intake.

Pointers to prevent dehydration

Normally, all of us lose some body water every single day through sweat, urine, stool, tears, or even during ailments like fever, vomiting and diarrhoea. While this fluid loss gets replaced through the water in the food, the water that we lose through intense activity or hot and sultry weather, needs to be replaced through the intake of regular water or other water-based fluids. Here are a few tips to keep the lid tight on dehydration:

- Always pack a water bottle along when your child is going to school or for a day trip.
- Offer your child water every hour or so during hot weather.
- Offer an extra water bottle to your child if he is going to play an outdoor sport or perform any other physical activity. Insist on his drinking water before the start of the activity, during the activity at regular intervals and after the activity, to replenish the fluids lost through sweat.
- Offer plenty of water and other healthy fluids to your child when he is ill, especially if he has fever, vomiting and diarrhoea.
- In hot and humid weather, put a frozen ice-pop maker in the water bottle of your child to help him quench his thirst effectively.

- If plain water is boring and humdrum for your child, make the water-drinking ritual a tad bit exciting by adding fun flavours to it such as a dash of lemon juice, orange slices, watermelon cubes, freshly cut cucumbers or a sprig of mint.
- Drink water regularly in the presence of your child so that he mimics you till it becomes a habit with him.

Survey Takeaway: Kanika Kush insists on her son making a 'daily report' to her about the number of glasses of water he consumes per day. This diktat, according to her, has helped him to consume at least eight glasses of water as a daily habit.

So, don't rely on your child to come up to you asking for water every time his body needs it. Just offer the life-saving drink to him at regular intervals, much as you would be administering his meals each day.

GET OFF THE JUNK FOOD HABIT

The lure of junk food is so compelling for children today that getting them back to the fresh and healthy meals cooked at home, sometimes seems more challenging than counting the hair on your head. It's raining candies, cookies, burgers and doughnuts wherever they look. To add to the woes, there are drool-inducing images all around them. Junk food is a pandemic that is here to stay, and children all around the globe are falling easy prey to it. The fallout? Children as young as middle schoolers are grappling with illnesses, such as diabetes, hypertension, growth retardation, obesity, reduced attention span, lack of energy and digestive tract disorders. The list of health problems is ever-growing.

So, what's there in these foods that makes them so unhealthy? It is the 'fearsome four': sugar, salt, fat and refined flour (maida). Individually or together, they hijack the taste buds of the hapless children. In the garb of enhancing the taste of food, this deadly quartet hooks children (why forget adults?) on to these foods, getting them grievously addicted. This junk pile of food is either laden with tons of saturated fat, excessive salt, dollops of sugar, or made with refined flour; and in the worst scenario, with all the four. They definitely make the food more appetizing, but at a huge cost of lifestyle diseases.

Let's unmask these wily offenders by going through each profile, so that we can identify them, and get our children out of their strong clutches:

1. Foods with sugar

Some foods are loaded with sugar. Excess sugar in the body gets stored as body fat in the liver and muscles, leading to the risk of obesity, type II diabetes, digestion problems, tooth decay and heart diseases. Sugar goes by various names, such as table sugar, corn syrup, brown sugar, maple syrup, molasses, agave nectar and invert syrup. Foods with these names as part of the ingredient list are all unhealthy. They aggravate sugar-cravings further, leading to a binge cycle.

Common offenders:

- cakes, pastries and doughnuts
- cookies
- chocolates
- sweets and candies
- sweetened sodas and other beverages

- ice cream and sorbets
- sugar-sweetened milkshakes
- canned fruit juices
- most desserts

Assumed-healthy-but-loaded-with-sugar foods:

- candied dried fruits, such as cranberries, kiwifruit and apricot (have added sugar syrup)
- sauces and spreads like coleslaw, barbecue sauce, ketchup, commercially made peanut butter
- breakfast cereals (including many whole grain ones) like fruit loops, sugar-coated flakes/loops and candied crisps
- packaged flavoured fruit yogurt
- most health bars, energy bars and protein bars
- most commercially available energy drinks, sports drinks and flavoured water, etc.

A caveat: Sugar is sold with numerous names as mentioned above. So, make sure that you scan the ingredient label for hidden sugar names. Also, ensure that sugar doesn't figure in the top three ingredients of the food that you're looking to buy.

2. Foods with bad fats

There are good fats and there are bad fats. While good fats (polyunsaturated and monounsaturated fats) are essential for many bodily functions as discussed earlier, saturated fats have to be used very sparingly and trans-fats are best left alone. Both saturated and trans-fats can jack up bad cholesterol levels, clog arteries and increase the risk of heart disease in adulthood. In fact, unlike a few saturated fats that are good for health, trans-fats have no nutritive value at all. They raise bad cholesterol levels (LDL) and cause inflammation in the body.

Foods with saturated fats:

- red meat
- poultry with skin
- processed meats like sausages, bacon, salami
- full fat dairy (full fat milk, creamy cheese, butter, sour cream)
- ice cream
- palm oil, palm kernel oil
- cream-based dips, toppings, sandwich spreads and dressings, such as mayonnaise and Caesar dressing

Foods with saturated fats must be used sparingly.

Some important saturated fat facts are:

All fats are not created equal. Some saturated fats are actually healthy, as they may have a protective effect against cardiovascular disease (CVD). These are dairy products such as ghee, yogurt and paneer, and coconut oil. In fact, full fat dairy is good for children who are underweight.

Always check the nutrition labels for information on saturated fat or 'sat fat' as it may be named. 1.5 g or lower per 100 g of food serving is low; between 1.5 g and 5 g per 100 g of food serving is medium; and anything beyond 5 g per 100 g of food serving is high.

Trans-fats

Trans-fats must be avoided completely. They're in high demand, as they enhance the flavour of foods, making them crusty and crunchy. They even cost less and are added to foods in the stores to increase their shelf life. Trans-fats are found in:

- all deep-fried foods, such as French fries, pooris, pakodas, nuggets, fish fingers, chips, potato wedges and crumbed chicken
- processed and frozen foods, like packet cake mixes, heat-and-eat pizzas and frozen dinners, microwave popcorn packs with pre-added fat
- hydrogenated oils and foods containing these
- margarine, shortenings and lard
- blended vegetable oils
- many desserts that require oils and other fats, such as cakes, doughnuts, muffins and cream rolls
- commercially baked fast foods, such as burgers, pizzas, hotdogs, cakes, pies, doughnuts, waffles, croissants, crackers, cookies
- popcorn served in cinemas
- non-dairy coffee creamers
- peanut butter with hydrogenated oils
- many granola bars with hydrogenated oils

Some trans fat facts

Many of us may not be aware and it's very important to know that, most restaurants prepare food in hydrogenated oils to enhance flavours.

When oils are reused for cooking, trans fat content shoots up alarmingly.

Many food labels list trans-fats as 0 g on their labels. But this can be very misleading. Manufacturers can legally list any amount of trans fat below 1 g as 0 g. It could even be 0.9 g, being shown as 0 g. And as per the admissible quantity of trans-fats in the daily diet, these are considerable amounts.

3. Foods with excessive salt

Eating salt within recommended limits may be a good thing for the body, as salt has its own set of virtues, such as helping the body to maintain electrolyte balance; regulating body fluid and blood pressure; enabling proper functioning of the nervous system; and supporting proper contraction and relaxation of muscles. The problem arises when we rattle the salt shaker a wee bit too hard! Too much salt is one of the primary causes of begetting some lifestyle illnesses, like hypertension, water retention and kidney issues.

Popular sodium offenders

- frozen, processed or packaged foods like sausages, bacon, salami, fish canned in brine, chicken nuggets, frozen dinners, microwave popcorn packs and packaged salted snacks, which use salt as a preservative
- popcorn served in cinemas
- processed cheese
- most commercially available sauces, ketchup, toppings, fillings and spreads
- pickles
- packaged soups
- nachos/tortilla chips with cheese dip
- potato chips
- pizzas and burgers
- French fries
- breakfast cereals

Some salty facts

Salt is composed of two minerals, sodium and chloride. Table salt contains about 40 per cent of sodium and 60 per cent of chloride. Sodium and salt should not be confused with each other, especially when looking at daily recommended quantities.

Most of us, including children, consume much more sodium than is required on a daily basis. The American Heart Association recommends a maximum limit of 2,300 mg of sodium per day. One teaspoon of salt contains this amount.

Seventy-five per cent of salt that is generally consumed by us per day, is 'hidden' in the processed foods that we buy. Always read product labels before you buy any food items off the shelf.

Himalayan sea salt is a better sodium option, as it is an unrefined salt with about eighty trace minerals. However, the sodium content of both table salt and Himalayan sea salt may be the same. Therefore, you still need to contain the salt consumption of your child, whether it is regular table salt or Himalayan sea salt.

The maximum recommended amount of salt for babies and children as per the American Heart Association, is:

- up to 12 months – less than 1 g of salt a day (less than 0.4 g of sodium)
- 1 to 3 years – 2 g of salt a day (0.8 g of sodium)
- 4 to 6 years – 3 g of salt a day (1.2 g of sodium)
- 7 to 10 years – 5 g of salt a day (2 g of sodium)
- 11 years and over – 6 g of salt a day (2.4 g of sodium)

4. Foods with refined flour

Also known as all-purpose flour or maida, this definitely isn't something you could trust your health with. It is a simple carbohydrate or a refined starch, which is stripped of its bran and germ, and is capable of wreaking havoc on the body.

The processing that it undergoes, renders it worthless, leaving it without the all-essential fibre and other nutrients, such as B vitamins, iron, magnesium, selenium and phosphorous. A regular consumption of this carbohydrate can cause a host of health problems, like obesity, type II diabetes, inflammation, gastrointestinal (GI) distress, constipation, colon cancer, heart ailments, etc.

Popular refined flour offenders

- breads and bread-based products such as bagels, sandwiches, wraps, pitas, rolls, croquettes and French toasts
- white pasta and noodles
- burgers, pizzas and hotdogs
- refined baked foods like cakes, doughnuts, cookies, biscuits, rusk and muffins
- pancakes and crepes
- white pasta sauce
- refined flour-based soups, such as cream of mushroom/asparagus/tomato/broccoli/spinach soup, creamy onion soup and corn chowder soup
- Indian dishes made of refined flour, such as bhatura, samosa, kachori, gulab jamun, kulcha, namak pade, gujia and vada pao

Some refined flour facts

Refined carbohydrates are less satiating than complex carbohydrates. They are digested by the body rather rapidly, and this leads to quick and successive blood sugar spikes, resulting in raised insulin levels. The outcome? You're hungry soon again! You end up bingeing and the vicious cycle continues till your stomach protests. This causes quick weight gain.

It is very easy to overeat refined flour-based foods because of their enhanced palatability and also because they don't require much chewing. Many of them being 'domino foods' have become staples for children these days, as they're highly addictive.

Refined flour is a major cause of acidity that can cause health problems, such as chronic inflammation, stomach ulcers, gastroesophageal reflux disease (GERD) and arthritis during adulthood.

Most breads are made of refined flour. Even if some of them are labelled as 'whole wheat bread' or 'whole grain bread', they may be partly containing refined flour. So, never buy bread without checking its list of ingredients. If a rye bread or a whole wheat bread or any other 'healthier bread' lists white flour/refined wheat flour/enriched flour/all-purpose flour/refined starch/maida on its ingredient list, you need to strike it off your grocery list, as these are all synonyms for refined flour.

Survey Takeaway: Eighty per cent of the parents that I surveyed, reported that their children loved junk food and it was a sheer challenge to curb this regular onslaught of unwholesome foods. Some families out of the ones surveyed, even resorted to eating three to four outside meals (restaurant/home delivery/take away) per week.

If your child is habituated to eating junk food, it is not just excessive sugar and salt, unhealthy fats and refined grains that you should be losing sleep over. Junk foods are also full of artificially added colours, flavours, preservatives and additives that are added to enhance taste and extend shelf life. Moreover, children generally pair junk food with aerated and sweetened drinks. The resultant meal can aptly be called 'a toxic, calorie-laden junk heap'. And eating outside food often is the surest way to load up on this junk pile.

Survey Takeaway: Seema Dabwal, whose son is 10 years old, says, 'We used to eat out a couple of times a week in the past and even stocked packaged foods. Over a period of time, we realized that it didn't go well with our digestive system. We suffered from heartburn and our body would feel bloated. While the experience of eating outside food was fun in that moment, the feeling that followed was anything but fun! So, I have eliminated packaged foods containing sugar and preservatives, including bread, ketchup and jam completely from my kitchen. We have stopped eating out completely, and I derive great pleasure from cooking fresh food for my child, food that is brimming with my love and is full of healing power and good energy!'

EATING HEALTHY GRATIFIES THE GREY CELLS

Providing your child with a proper balance of nutrients in their foundational years is absolutely crucial for the optimal development and functioning of the brain. Deficiency of certain nutrients in these formative years can play havoc on a child's cognitive growth, which may even show up in the form of falling school grades.

The nutrients which are absolutely essential for a child's cognitive growth are:

Iron: Iron plays a very crucial role in the development of the brain during the early years, impacting cognitive growth in a major way. The consequences of iron deficiency are grave in children and can be irreversible. It can cause anaemia, which can lead to attention-deficit disorder (ADD), severely affecting the IQ of a child. Make sure that your child's diet has adequate iron to meet their intellectual needs. The best food sources of iron are: organ meats; seafood; fish like salmon and sardines; eggs; dried beans; dried fruits like apricots, figs and prunes; vegetables like spinach, potato with skin and white button mushrooms; soybean; seeds of pumpkin and sesame; lentils; oatmeal and fortified cereal with 3.5 mg or more of iron per serve.

Iodine: Iodine deficiency, again, has dire consequences, and can be irreversible if ignored. This nutrient deficiency can cause a cognitive disorder called psychomotor development retardation (slowing down of thinking and movements) and cretinism which can impair intelligence, lower the attention span and delay cognitive and motor development. Iodine deficiency is found to be the world's paramount cause of mental retardation. The best food sources of iodine are: iodized salt; dairy like milk, yogurt, cheese; fish like tuna, sardines, salmon; eggs; prunes; lima beans and potatoes with skin.

Zinc: Deficiency of zinc can lead to impaired cognitive ability in the form of reduced attention span and diminished mental capacity. The best food sources are: meats; seafood; dried beans; seeds of hemp and pumpkin; yogurt; vegetables like spinach and shiitake mushrooms; cashews and fortified breakfast cereals with 3.8 mg of zinc per serve.

Choline: This nutrient aids memory development and other essential brain functions by increasing the production of stem cells. Foods rich in choline are: chicken breast; salmon; eggs;

peanuts and cruciferous vegetables such as cabbage, cauliflower and broccoli.

Essential fats: These good fats (especially DHA) also enhance the performance of the brain. The best food sources are: fish; seafood; eggs; chicken breast; soybeans; walnuts and seeds like chia seeds, flaxseeds and hemp seeds.

Water: It is one of the most indispensable nutrients that our body needs to function efficiently. Nearly three-fourths of the brain is composed of water, which makes this life-giving liquid the chief component for the smooth functioning of the brain. When dehydration occurs due to reduced consumption of water, the brain releases a stress hormone called cortisol. Cortisol constricts the brain cells, leading to fatigue, mental lethargy, irritability and clouded thinking. So, make sure that your child irrigates their grey cells adequately by drinking at least eight glasses of water every day at regular intervals.

While the above-mentioned nutrients are the brain's closest allies, there are some more foods that boost memory, concentration, academic performance and ameliorate overall brain health. These are fruits like: berries (all varieties), musk melon, banana and apple; vegetables like sweet potato, carrot, pumpkin and kale, and dried beans like black-eyed peas.

With so many unhealthy and tantalizing options all around, healthy eating may be nothing short of a battleground for parents. But mealtimes don't always have to be frustrating and exasperating. You just need to hang in there and keep trying! Remember, it's the child's palate that you're training, so expect the ride to be a little bumpy!

TIPS TO ENSURE THAT GOOD HEALTH BECOMES A HABIT

Be a positive role model: Eat healthy on a regular basis and let your child watch you eat. He is sure to follow suit soon.

Make meals a family affair: Family meals are powerful. Eating at least one meal a day as a family can have an immense effect on your child's habits. Children are more likely to eat the foods they generally don't fancy if they observe their whole family eating them. The relaxed ambience and conversations help children unwind and be more flexible.

Involve your child in the process: It's good to involve them now and then in the meal-making process. Take your child grocery shopping; involve him in washing veggies and fruits; ask him to assist in laying the table, and so on. Inclusive activities like these can raise his sense of self-worth and awareness about what foods he eats.

Ditch distractions: Eating mindfully without unnecessary distractions helps form positive connections with food. Children are more aware of the flavours, aromas and textures of the food when they eat without the blaring TV to distract them. It also relays the message to your child that these meals are important to you as exclusive family time.

Be creative, it pays dividends: Use your imagination to offer offbeat (not necessarily complicated) dishes that may appeal to your child's taste buds. You could cook the usual dishes differently, or change the way you present them to renew his curiosity. Believe me, this works wonders! Some handy pointers in this direction are:

- Cut foods into various fun shapes.
- Use a variety of brightly coloured fruits and vegetables.
- Assign dishes playful names.
- Experiment with textures.
- Use attractive and vibrant dishes and bowls, perhaps with your child's favourite cartoon or superhero characters on them.

Give conditional choices: Hand over some control to the child by giving her conditional choices. Instead of asking your child an open-ended question, like 'What would you like to eat?' ask her 'What would you like to eat tonight: broccoli or beans?' When you give her a choice between two healthy foods, you're in a win-win situation.

Praise a little, it doesn't hurt: Praise your child when she eats the food that she generally creates a fuss over. Positive feedback encourages children to repeat desirable behaviour.

De-junk your kitchen cabinets: Out of sight is out of mind. When you stop stocking unhealthy snacks and replace them with healthier options, children adapt to the new regime after the initial hue and cry.

Serve meals on time, every day: Ensure that your child eats her meals on time and at regular intervals. Long gaps between meals can cause lethargy and brain fog.

Make breakfast non-negotiable: Never let your child skip breakfast. A good breakfast, consisting of a mix of complex carbohydrates and proteins, will keep her energy levels high for most of the day.

Keep healthy foods handy: Keep healthy snacks like fruits, dried fruits, nuts or homemade trail-mix handy. This will dissuade children from gorging on junk food that can trigger rapid blood sugar spikes and crashes leading to fatigue.

Educate your child: Teach your child about the benefits of eating healthy. You could use storybooks or make up stories about her favourite superhero eating vegetables and fruits to become stronger. You could even use role-play or props like glossy food charts with colourful pictures to explain.

Never bribe with food rewards: Bribing your child with, 'I'll get you a blueberry muffin, if you finish your spinach,' will not work in the long term. This approach would lead to negative associations with foods they're being bribed to eat. It will also turn them into manipulative little beings. Giving them occasional non-food rewards like extra play time in the park, should work just fine.

Allow occasional indulgence: There are just too many junk food stimuli around children to resist today, and a whole lot of negative peer pressure to give in to eating unhealthy foods. An occasional indulgence with their favourite meals helps them stay on a healthy regime for the rest of the days.

Remember, your child's eating habits aren't going to change overnight. You need to be patient and keep trying. Your persistence will definitely yield results in due time. The small steps that you take each day in this direction, will not only help your child with their growth spurts, mental development and physical energy, but will also promote a lifetime of healthy eating.

7

Inner Calm Through Mindfulness

'Children are natural zen masters; their world is brand new in each and every moment.'

JOHN BRADSHAW, EDUCATOR AND SPEAKER

THERE IS SO much sensory overload in a child's life today that it can be truly inundating and nerve-wracking at times. Children's lives are crammed with so many things that they're moving at a breakneck tempo in life. In addition to the dizzying bulk of school-related pressures, children are expected to excel in all the other areas as well.

This hurricane of incessant activities is making them painfully high-strung. There's no time to pause, breathe, realign and restart. In the process, children never get to experience the bouncy-breezy, happy-go-lucky childhood which should deservedly be theirs for as long as they are children. Hence, they need periodic access to interventions that can help them alleviate anxiety. Making them mindful is a great way of helping them claim back their elusive inner peace.

Mindfulness is a state of being fully aware of what one is doing: a state of 'being present' in the moment. In this state of heightened focus, where the mind is not distracted with the issues of the past or the worries of the future, the brain is able to recalibrate itself to its default mode. It is a meditative exercise, where a person focuses on the 'here and now' by paying attention to their breathing. Mindfulness is believed to be the panacea for many modern-day illnesses.

POSITIVE EFFECTS OF PRACTISING MINDFULNESS

- improves focus, concentration and decision-making abilities;
- allays anxiety, reduces the chances of depression and helps children develop a more positive outlook in life;
- brings about self-awareness, which boosts their self-confidence;
- equips children with better coping skills by teaching them self-management of stressful emotions, like anger, fear and frustration;
- helps children pause and think before responding instantly, which helps them to better understand other's feelings and points of view;
- helps enhance the quality of sleep and reduce the time taken to fall asleep.

EIGHT GREAT WAYS TO PRACTISE MINDFULNESS

1. **Belly breathing:** Ask your child to lie flat on his back and place his hand on his belly. Ask him to breathe in and out, and make him pay attention only to how his hand and belly move

up and down. Instruct him to focus on his breathing and count each breath. Belly breathing automatically triggers an easing up response in the body that helps children relax. Set a few minutes aside in a day for this relaxation activity to help your child unwind.

2. **Journaling:** It is an extraordinary technique for children and adults alike, with remarkable long-lasting effects. From the mindfulness perspective, it is a great tool for children to release their emotions in a healthy manner, which helps calm their mental chatter, deal better with challenges in daily life and gain self-awareness. It can serve as a cooling-off time in their day in a big way.

   Encourage your child to maintain a notebook, notepad or a folder to write at least a page or two every day after dinner or before bedtime. Prompt him to write down a minimum of five things that he is grateful for that day, besides of course writing just about anything that comes to mind initially. When children jot down all the good things that happen to them each day, it deepens the feeling of gratitude in them for all the positive things bestowed in their lives.

3. **Visualization:** It is a self-guided activity that involves forming mental images of what one wants, and then focusing on each of these images slowly, positively and frame by frame in the manner that one wants it all to happen. As described lucidly by Jack Canfield in his book, *The Success Principles*, visualization is 'the act of creating compelling and vivid pictures in your mind...it activates the creative powers of your subconscious mind...focuses your brain to notice available resources that were always there but were

previously unnoticed…visualization simply makes the brain achieve more.'

Visualization can help release anger, fear, hurt and other stressful emotions. It can help a child recalibrate their mind to make things that were stressful appear easy or less frustrating. For instance, if your child is feeling unsettled about an upcoming exam, teach her to close her eyes and visualize herself preparing diligently for the exam without being tense and doing well in the exam. Encourage her to visualize whenever she is too stressed out about anything in her life.

Survey Takeaway: For Kaashik Bansal, it was easier to introduce his preschooler to visualization and meditation, as he himself has been practising various forms of spiritual healing for many years now. He says, 'My son and I start our healing sessions with a daily prayer of gratitude followed by visualization. We visualize planet Earth with closed eyes… imagining peace, happiness, joy, lots of greenery and clean air on Earth. We imagine family, friends and other people around us being happy and tranquil. This daily practice has helped my son, since the tender age of 3 years, to realize that there are positive energies and vibrations in the Universe, and that such positive thoughts play a huge role in helping us transform ourselves inside out. He is 7 years old now, and this intervention has given him a sense of humility and inner calm. Today, he even leads me and his other friends in prayers, and also helps me in my healing sessions that I conduct for others as a hobby.'

Jack Canfield explains in his book, *The Success Principles for Teens*, that the principle of visualization also applies to learning anything new. He writes, 'A Harvard University study proved that students who visualized in advance performed tasks with nearly 100 per cent accuracy, while students who didn't visualize, achieved only 55 per cent accuracy.' Olympic athletes and other professional sportspersons from various parts of the globe have been employing visualization techniques to optimize their performance.

4. **Mindful nature walk:** Take a trail walk or just a walk in the park with your child. Help her notice her surroundings keenly with the help of all her primal senses while maintaining mindful silence. Let her observe the shape of leaves; touch them and feel them; smell the wonderful fragrance of flowers and listen to the birds chirping. Let your child lead the way through this leisurely walk at her own pace.

5. **Mindful eating:** Most children eat hurriedly and mindlessly these days, as they're either preoccupied with too many random thoughts during meal times, or they're watching TV or some other screen while eating. In the process, food doesn't get the focus it deserves, despite being the primary source of nourishment for the body. You can help change things for the better, by encouraging your child to eat at least one meal/snack per day with full mindfulness. You can serve your child's favourite food for him to practise mindful eating. Ask him to eat it very slowly using the four senses of taste, sight, touch and smell, enjoying the flavour, texture and aroma of every bite he takes.

6. **Mindful melody sessions:** Encourage your child to listen to his favourite music by focussing completely on its subtleties,

like rhythm, beat, tempo, melody, pitch and distinctness of each instrument. During these mindful music sessions, ensure that your child doesn't multitask, as this can relegate music to the background. Also, there are a whole lot of musical compositions made specially to improve mindfulness. These are based on certain therapeutic sounds, such as raindrops, ocean waves, thunderstorms, chirping of birds, flutes, Tibetan bowls, etc. These are very effective in relaxing stressed-out minds.

Survey Takeaway: Ruby Singh says that 'we (she and her daughter) discovered, quite by accident, the Buddhist singing bowls, and sometimes both of us enjoy listening to them as a relaxing activity.' She is even considering downloading the Headspace meditation app to practise simple guided meditation together with her daughter.

7. **Yoga:** Introducing yoga into the lives of children can help alleviate depression and anxiety, and enhance self-awareness. Yoga asanas, along with pranayama (deep breathing yoga), are a great tool to blunt the blow of stress on children, and help them connect back to the 'here and now'. It is best to get them to learn yoga under the supervision of a good instructor.

8. **Digital detox**: Getting children off all types of screens for a full day or half a day can also help them reconnect with their immediate environment in a mindful manner. You could use this time to explore a positive activity, such as a creative hobby, playing a mentally challenging game or reading a book together.

In his book, *The Power of Habit*, Charles Duhigg says that keystone habits are the 'small changes or habits that people introduce into their routines, that unintentionally carry over into other aspects of their lives'.

Think of these interventions as keystone habits that will not only calm your child, but will also help in their overall growth.

8

Life Skills

*'Chance never helps those who
do not help themselves.'*

SOPHOCLES, ANCIENT GREEK PLAYWRIGHT

LIFE SKILLS ARE the skills that help a person to deal with the various challenges of life in an effective manner. These are the few vital skills that will give your child an edge throughout their life. While many of them may appear simple and mundane, their cumulative benefit over a lifetime is tremendous. It is unfortunate that many parents are not aware of the importance of life skills.

As Jim Rohn says, 'What is easy to do is also easy not to do.'

We owe it to our children to make them self-reliant. Equipping them with some basic skills will also make them more confident adults with a strong sense of self-worth.

It's prudent to start early, as it's easier to teach some of these skills to a child rather than to an adult. Children do not have mental blocks or fears that come with age. So, catch them young and see them soar!

Survey Takeaway: Like so many others, Seema Dabwal too grew up witnessing her mother, grandmother and all the other women in the family carry out the household chores. Boys in her extended family had a tough time living away from home for further studies or professional engagements, as they couldn't cope with household chores. When she had her son, she made up her mind that she would teach him various home-based life skills and make him self-reliant and independent. Since he turned 4, she started involving him in simple chores such as changing his clothes himself after school, putting them in the laundry basket, keeping his shoes and school bag in their stipulated places, etc. Now, as a 10-year-old, he helps his mom in household chores, such as making the bed, watering the plants, setting the dinner table, folding washed clothes and even dusting the furniture when the house-help is on leave.

In the following sections, I have covered the top ten life skills that I feel are crucial to learn, not only to be able to survive in this world, but also to lead a fulfilling life.

1. Public speaking

*'My public speaking course was arguably
the best investment I made in my life.'*

WARREN BUFFET, BUSINESS MAGNATE AND PHILANTHROPIST

The significance of public speaking as a life skill is often overlooked. It is one skill that is very crucial for acquiring a well-rounded personality. It helps students to speak confidently in a public space, be it at school or in front of a group. Besides, it also helps them as adults, especially at work.

Important benefits of public speaking:

Increases confidence: It would endow children with self-assurance and confidence when they're required to address the class or the whole school. It will help them tremendously in the future when they have to present a report or speak at a conference. It also comes in handy for children who aspire to dabble in extra-curricular activities, like elocution, recitation, debating and theatre.

Sharpens communication skills: When your child grows into an adult, it will help her make headway in the professional arena. In the world of extreme competition, effective communication skills help tremendously in clearing interviews, making a sales pitch, winning business deals, moving up the corporate ladder, and so on. Apart from the workplace, clear, confident and persuasive articulation can also enhance the quality of everyday life.

Helps build social connections: Public speaking helps shy and self-conscious individuals to get over their social anxiety, and make social and professional connections.

While public speaking comes easy and instinctively to some children, there are many others who feel unsettled at the thought of speaking, even in the presence of a single individual. For such a child, start with smaller steps at the beginning, such as taking her to the house of a close friend or a relative where she feels less conscious even in the presence of new people. Gradually, you could encourage her to participate in class presentations, debating and elocution competitions, by enrolling her in a summer camp. As parents, it is our responsibility to help them ease their angst early in life by offering them opportunities to learn effective public-speaking skills. But while doing so, always ensure that your child enjoys an opportunity to speak in front of others, and is not feeling pressurized to perform in order to appease anybody else.

2. Vocabulary building

Having a good vocabulary can be very crucial in developing literary skills which will not only help a child gain success in school, but also during their adult years. Having a good vocabulary is the best indicator of success in academics. Parents play a significant role in a child's early years to help them build a rich vocabulary. Children learn to communicate by listening to their parents. If you have conversations at home that involve new and unfamiliar words every day, your child is sure to expand his vocabulary rapidly. You could name new objects (new for him), emotions, qualities of a person or action words every day in their correct context while talking to your child. Another way of enriching your child's vocabulary is through reading out books to him when he is young, and to encourage him to read a variety of books all through his growing-up years. The more reading variety a child is exposed to, the better his word bank becomes. (More details in the 'Intellectual Growth' chapter). Also, grown-up children should be encouraged to read the editorial section of the daily newspaper and look up the dictionary for words that they do not comprehend. Playing word games verbally or playing certain board games and activities, such as Scrabble, Hangman, Boggle and crossword puzzles, also amplifies a child's vocabulary in a big way. As mentioned earlier in the book, introduce the daily activity of learning a word/thought of the day, with new words or phrases introduced every day.

Lifelong benefits of building vocabulary:

- Children with a good vocabulary generally have an academic edge over others in literacy subjects.
- It spruces up a child's oral as well as written communication skills, both of which are crucial for success in life and at work.
- It bolsters a child's ability to express ideas and thoughts more effectively.
- It enhances a child's knowledge base, helping them learn more extensively about the world.
- It helps tremendously in clearing entrance tests, such as SAT and GMAT.

3. Touch-typing

Touch-typing or keyboarding, as it is popularly known, is a very crucial skill in this day and age. Touch-typing is the ability to use muscle memory to find keys fast without using the sense of sight, and with all the available fingers. Computers have almost replaced actual writing with pen on a paper, with the ubiquitous keyboard. While I think it is important to get children into the habit of writing with a pen every day (however little), the importance of touch-typing just can't be undermined. A child who has acquired keyboard dexterity will be armed with confidence to use technology to her advantage throughout her academic years as well as her professional life, since she is likely to spend thousands of hours on the keyboard during her lifetime.

Learning the 'ten finger typing' skill will give a major head start to your child at school and in her adult life. With extensive typing practice over the school years, your child can pick up a good speed, which will help her become more productive with her typing time. Typing dexterously will also arm her with confidence on being able to perform literacy-based work efficiently. Touch-typing really comes in handy when one has to write research papers online, submit online assignments, compose thousands of emails over a lifetime, and for a lot more. An accomplished touch-typist can type up to almost eighty words per minute without looking down at the keyboard with almost negligible errors. This speed can save a big chunk of time for a person, compared to an untrained typist, adding to their efficiency and productivity in a big way. It is one of the best productivity tools that you can arm your child with to save her hundreds of hours over her entire life.

Some of the good online touch-typing tutors are Typing. com, Typesy, Mavis Beacon, UltraKey 6 and Speed Typing Online.

4. Basic financial management

Basic money management skills are so critical to navigate life that they have to be taught to children sooner than you think they need to know. Surprisingly, most schools do not include this in their curricula.

You have to drill it into their minds and get them into the habit of managing money and saving at a young age. To facilitate this, you can start by fixing a task-based monthly or daily allowance for children, for helping with household chores, such as making beds, helping with laundry, setting the table for dinner, etc. Not only will this teach children how to start saving, but will also teach them how to share household responsibilities and become more independent.

As soon as children start drawing an allowance from home, you can kick-start your lessons in money management. In fact, children as young as 3 years can grasp basic concepts of money.[32]

According to a study conducted by the University of Cambridge, money habits are formed in children by the time they're 7 years old.[33] Help them maintain two separate piggy banks or envelopes, one for 'spendings' and the other for 'savings'. When your child receives money in the form of rewards for chores, winning prizes and parting/birthday gifts from relatives, ask him to divide and put money equally in both his 'banks'. Let him spend from the 'spendings' piggy bank for his petty needs, but encourage him to save the 'savings' money for bigger and more expensive gifts that he desires. This approach will add excitement to the whole idea of saving money.

By the time children turn 10, having 'saved' for a couple of years by then, they can be taught the concept of compound interest and a few simple calculations.

Albert Einstein describes compound interest interestingly: 'Compound interest is the eighth wonder of the world. He who understands it, earns it...he who doesn't...pays it.'

You can also teach the concept of delayed gratification, and then encourage them to have a slightly longer-term goal for their savings. These savings could be for a bigger toy/game or a new sports kit. Introduce them to the concept of 'comparison shopping' around the age of 6.[34] Comparison shopping is the practice of comparing prices of goods provided by different shops before making a purchase in order to get the best deal. By the time they turn 12, they should be able to understand the concept of a savings bank account and its significance in simple terms.

Around the ages of 14 to 15, you should be able to explain to them about how a bank works in the fields of savings and investments. Now is also the right time to make them understand the importance of spending within the family's means.

By the time they're 18, you should have given them enough life lessons on money management to enable them to grasp the concept of what is an asset versus a liability, to have a separate bank account of their own, to be able to operate their bank account and to be able to use credit/debit cards responsibly. Your constant and consistent pep-talks about financial prudence should have drilled into them the importance of being thrifty and becoming smart savers by now.

By teaching your child the fundamentals of financial awareness and prudence, you're laying a solid foundation of smart financial management for him in the years to come, that will hold him in good stead when he eventually flies out of your nest.

5. Personal hygiene

While younger children's hygiene is regularly supervised by adults to a great extent, it's the teens who need a push from time to time to maintain regular hygiene. Sometimes, it could just be their collective mindset that makes them underrate the importance of brushing their teeth regularly or taking a shower daily. Even at the cost of appearing pesky to your teen, you have to keep the pressure on to ensure that he doesn't skip his daily ablutions. Children who live in residential campuses (especially undergraduate/postgraduate students) are likely to need self-discipline even more, in the absence of parental guidance. The same applies to children who take up their first jobs far from home.

Poor hygiene is a big reason why children fall prey to certain aches, allergies and illnesses, such as:

- dental cavities
- head lice
- typhoid
- diarrhoea
- scabies
- boils and ringworms
- gum diseases like gingivitis
- herpes
- chlamydia
- urinary tract infection (UTI)
- athlete's foot

Some not-so-serious-yet-offensive fallouts of not maintaining personal hygiene are bad breath, plaque build-up in teeth and offensive body odour.

In order for children to be guarded against diseases while away from home, you need to give them regular hygiene peptalks. Even better would be to start when they're very young, and continue to advise them (even if unsolicited) through their teenage years, till it becomes a habit that continues into adulthood.

Maintaining good hygiene helps keep illnesses at bay. Impeccable personal grooming greatly enhances self-image, self-esteem and self-confidence.

6. Basic cooking

Cooking is one of the most critical life skills needed to survive independently. Acquiring basic cooking skills can come in handy in the future, not only for girls but for boys as well. I know a lot of young adults who live independently, who struggle to manage three healthy meals a day for themselves. Many of them can't afford a cook, nor can they cook a meal on their own.

The fallout? They have to rely on unhealthy takeaways or 'heat and eat' processed foods with questionable nutritive value. One doesn't have to compete with Gordon Ramsay or Jamie Oliver to be able to manage perfectly palatable and healthy meals for oneself. Cooking doesn't necessarily have to be complicated to be gratifying to the palate. There are enough recipes that are quick to cook, yet savoury to eat.

An age-wise breakdown of kitchen-tasks and cooking: I am grouping children by age ranges so that it is easy for you to match your child's skill levels with the age-specific tasks, keeping the child's safety in handling kitchen work in mind. Note that learning these skills would also depend on each child's individual learning pace.

Preschoolers (4–5 years)

Low-risk tasks under constant supervision of an adult could include:

- rinsing fruits and vegetables
- stirring and whisking batter
- mashing soft foods
- spreading butter and other spreads
- cutting soft fruits and vegetables with a plastic knife

Junior schoolers (6–8 years)

Still very young to handle cooking, they could handle the following tasks:

- use cookie/pizza cutters
- whisk and whip eggs, batter and liquids
- peel fruits and vegetables with a plastic peeler

Pre-teens (9–12 years)

- use a food processor, smoothie maker and a blender
- pare fruits and vegetables with a real knife and peeler
- cook rice in a rice-cooker
- make sandwiches, salads and smoothies under supervision
- use appliances like a hand-mixer, microwave and toaster

Teenagers (13–16 years)

This age group can manage most kitchen tasks and some cooking independently.

- use small and big knives
- peel, slice and grate fruits and vegetables
- chop, dice and mince
- grate cheese and vegetables with a hand grater
- fry eggs
- grill food
- bake cookies, breads, muffins, etc.
- sauté, pan fry, grill and roast food
- knead dough
- marinate foods
- cook simple meals for the family

Young adults (16 upwards)

Children who are 16 years and above can handle all cooking along with the preparation, just like adults.

Advantages of introducing children to basic cooking while they're young:

- they will grow up into responsible and self-sufficient adults.

- they feel a sense of accomplishment which bolsters their self-confidence.
- they're more likely to eat a large variety of healthier foods.
- they're likely to become hosts and entertain their guests, a skill that is much needed in today's world.
- they're likely to not have a false sense of entitlement and respect those who perform the job of cooking in their lives.

7. Sex education

Sex education is way too critical as a life skill to be ignored or postponed. Proper sex education reiterated at different stages of a child's growing years, is extremely important for their physical and emotional well-being, and can have lasting effects on their adult life. As children grow up, sex education becomes more complex, and should cover topics like individual sexuality, intimate relationships, reproduction, sexual diseases, delayed sexual gratification and the dangers of unprotected sex.

It's just too easy in today's world for a child to glean information on sex. Whether you like it or not, a child's exposure in this field begins much earlier than you would want it to start. They learn about sex from their friends at school and at sleepovers, from surfing the Internet and by watching TV. The worrisome part is that what they learn from these external sources could be half-baked and misleading. The information from some of these sources can portray sex in a very superficial, sensational, reckless or frivolous way. And, this can be really degrading and unwholesome for a child's psyche.

So, by being her first source of information on everything to do with sex, you're ensuring that she gets the essential inputs in the right perspective. Through these conversations where there would be many questions from her side, and proper (and age-appropriate) responses from your side, the child will get the feeling of comfort that she can talk to you about anything related to this topic, even if she is in a distressing predicament someday. You need to keep these sessions frequent and repetitive, with more information added at every physical growth milestone.

What is the right time to start?

We were a completely clueless set of parents in the initial parenting years, and hadn't given much thought to when and how to commence imparting sex education to our son. His first such question came as a bolt from the blue, leaving me totally off balance! I clearly remember the day when I was getting the evening snack ready for my 6-year-old, and he suddenly asked me, 'Mama, what is a condom?' To say that I was embarrassed would be an understatement. I was mortified! And I goofed-up! I muttered that there was no such word and he must have confused it for 'condemn' which meant 'criticize'. And he believed me, if only for a day, and then he felt betrayed for being lied to by his own parent. The rest, as they say, is history. That was a sign for me and my husband to strategize on when and how to educate our child proactively from time to time. And we did manage it fairly well. I remember using conversation starters, such as sighting a pregnant woman and seizing the opportunity to teach him about how babies are born. We always tried to answer his uncomfortable questions as honestly as possible in age-appropriate ways. If the query was too overwhelming for either of us, we would tell him that we weren't very sure of the answer and would find out soon and revert.

While I botched up in the beginning and got my act together a wee bit late, you could avoid such sticky situations by starting proactively when your child is a preschooler. You could start the education by teaching your child the name of all the parts of the body, including private parts, in a matter-of-fact manner. You also need to make your child understand that their body is absolutely private and out of bounds for outsiders to see or touch. Teach them the distinction between 'good touch' and 'bad touch', preferably through teachable moments or conversation starters to make the conversation a lot less awkward and abrupt. Teaching moments can show up in the form of a pregnant woman, a couple kissing on TV or an advertisement about sanitary pads, and so on. Pre-empt sex-related queries by practising responses to many such questions in order to be adequately prepared. If you're not sure of how to answer a question, there is no harm in saying that you're not too sure and that you will find out and answer.

By the time your child reaches puberty age, talk about the bodily changes that puberty brings. To your adolescent or teen, you could talk about the perils of early pregnancy, pornography and cybercrimes of a sexual nature. It is also very important to talk to them about how to manage peer pressure to indulge in sexual activities, and about sex in relation to emotions and relationships. It's very important that you speak to your teen proactively from time to time, to encourage them to trust you and talk to you in times of any sexual dilemma and difficulty.

Although most schools have sex education in the curriculum these days, it is prudent to personally ensure that your child gets the right perspective on this topic and you are their go-to person for any such queries.

8. Basic laundry

However well a person may be backed-up with domestic assistance, there will be many occasions in a boarding school, college or early adulthood when they may have to clean their clothes on their own. In such times, they will be faced with the choice to either wash their clothes or wear dirty clothes.

Such a phase could show up as soon as children leave the shelter of home to pursue their education or to join a job in another city or country. Knowledge of how to do basic laundry can come in handy then. I definitely think that children need to be taught how to wash, dry, hang, as well as iron their clothes.

This was one skill I somehow overlooked teaching my son during his childhood, and landed up texting an entire washing manual (well, literally) on WhatsApp, on how to wash his basic clothes (step by step). This was while he was in his first year of undergraduate studies, when the hostel washing machine decided to break down one day, creating panic amongst students (especially those who had exhausted all their clean clothes and were left with no choice but to hand-wash). It was difficult texting detailed instructions to a distressed young adult who behaved as if he were taking down instructions to build a rocket. I knew then, that basic laundry has to definitely make it to the 'what all parents need to teach their children' list.

Believe me, it's much easier to start teaching them when they're way younger and eager to learn a new skill. Just too many teenagers transition into adulthood without having a clue about how to wash their clothes, and find themselves 'stuck' in a situation.

Doing laundry has become much simpler than it was when I was a child. It's been reduced to almost a one-button-press chore with the washing machines humming in almost every household now.

Children as young as 6 can start assisting adults in the laundry process by sorting and separating dirty clothes, loading the washing machine, and folding their own clean and tiny clothes. They can gradually move up to pouring detergent into the washing machine as they get older, then run the washing machine without supervision, and finally, to be able to comfortably do the household laundry as a young teen. As teenagers, they can be given lessons in washing underclothes manually. Learning to iron clothes will need a little more supervision and a little more practice for them.

9. Riding a bicycle

Riding a bicycle is a life skill that your child may actually look forward to acquiring.

This is one skill that will stay with the child for life. It sure will entail a couple of benign falls and scraped knees and elbows during the initial days, but it is still worth it! Cycling is not only a great cardio exercise that children need, it's a great way to commute short distances for children and longer distances for adults. It can bestow a feeling of absolute freedom on children, as they don't have to be perpetually dependent on adults for every small errand, or to get to their play destination. And once they enter adulthood, spinning around comes with a whole range of benefits. This spinning machine's power cannot be underestimated. Some of its benefits are:

- It's a recreational activity that the whole family can take up together.
- It's a fun, low-cost and a fast means of moving around

and getting to places, as you can avoid traffic snarls easily.
- It's a fun way of working out and a low-impact exercise that packs the punch of cardio, endurance and strength training.
- It keeps many lifestyle illnesses at bay, such as heart ailments, diabetes, obesity and arthritis.
- It's a healthy, cheap and the most environment-friendly means of going to work every day.
- It releases adrenalin and endorphins that make it a great stress buster.
- It's a great way of making friends, as there are scores of cycling groups in almost every city these days.

The sooner you get them on a bicycle, the better it is for them. You can get them to learn riding ideally between the age of 3 and 5, as it's easier to learn to balance and gain confidence when they're this young. However, if you missed this milestone, worry not! It's never too late to get their wheels turning!

10. Swimming

Swimming is again a skill that every child should learn for its many positive applications in life. Once you learn to swim, you are unlikely to forget it. While a child can learn to swim on turning 1, there is no upper age limit to stop swimming. It benefits children as much as it benefits adults. In fact, it is one sport they can indulge in for as long as they live, as it's a low-impact sport.

Reasons why swimming is a life skill:

It can be a life-saver: This is the number one reason for children to learn swimming. Drowning is a very common cause of accidental death in children as well as in adults all over the globe. Whether you're at a beach with family or friends; at a pool party; in a boat that tips over; or however far-fetched as it may sound, in a ship that is sinking (remember the *Titanic*?), swimming can save your life. When a person is in a tricky predicament in and around water, knowing how to flip and float on their back and to swim to safety can save their life.

It opens the door to many other recreational activities: Knowing how to swim can lead a person to experience many other aquatic leisure activities and sports, such as water polo, triathlon, surfing, kayaking, canoeing, boat fishing and yachting.

It's a fabulous way to stay fit and healthy: Swimming is one of the few sports that exercise your entire body. It's a great form of cardio as well as strength training. And since it's a low-impact activity, it is highly recommended by doctors, even for senior citizens with joint pain and many other illnesses.

It is a great stress buster: Almost every swimmer swears by the unwinding effect that swimming has on the nerves and emotions. It can alleviate the day's stress like few other activities can.

Remember, it's never too late to learn to swim. So, find a pool near you, get hold of a good trainer and watch your child have fun splashing around! Join her to double the fun!

9

Detriments of Helicopter Parenting

'The trouble with learning to parent on the job is that your child is the teacher.'

ROBERT BRAULT, AUTHOR

HELICOPTER PARENTS, AS the name aptly conveys, typically hover above their children persistently, being overprotective and over-controlling. They are over-involved in making decisions on their behalf, resolving their disputes and taking more responsibility than is needed for their children's life events, specially their successes and failures.

As Dr Ann Dunnewold, a licensed psychologist and author of *Even June Cleaver Would Forget the Juice Box,* puts it, 'It means being involved in a child's life in a way that is over controlling, overprotecting, and over perfecting, in a way that is in excess of responsible parenting.' In short, they're so involved in their children's lives that it could be smothering their overall growth.

The 'I Will Never Let You Fail' Helicopter: The parents in this situation try to help children in most of their tasks, even when the children can manage these on their own. I know of cases where parents have even gone to the extent of trying to enforce who their child should room up with in a hostel. This micromanagement becomes completely counterproductive in today's harsh world. It is because children are bound to (and need to) face many challenges all throughout on their own, struggle while trying to overcome these, and eventually, become mature by doing so. Overprotection by parents can render them incapable of facing these challenges head-on and overcoming them with ease. Overparenting never allows children to grow out of their 'training wheels' and learn to balance themselves on the bicycle of life because the parents are afraid that the child may fall and bruise himself. They don't realize that children falling a few times and bruising themselves is an essential part of the learning process. This way, they will never really learn to be independent.

Over-protective parents often fear that their child may fail in some spheres of life, and may not be able to cope with the consequences. Failure could be in the form of low grades in exams, not being able to get the desired stream for graduation, not making it to the school sports team, not landing a coveted job, and likewise. You may worry that your child is not strong enough to handle such situations and may crumble with disappointment. Unfortunately, there is no awareness about the importance of letting your child be. It is precisely these situations that can teach your child coping skills, confidence and self-sufficiency. Helicopter parents are likely to be insecure in their outlook, and are obsessed by the desire to ensure that their children do not encounter any failure or negative situation. One of the biggest misconceptions amongst most parents is that it is by constantly prodding the child, will he succeed.

It is very normal for some parents to have experienced neglected childhoods, which can make them long to overcompensate for the vacuum in their past by being overly protective and involved in their children's lives. The unpleasant experiences of their own lives may compel them to hand-hold their children perpetually, with the fear that they might fall and hurt themselves if the figurative grip on their hands is loosened even a wee bit.

The 'You Must Continue the Family Legacy' Helicopter: There's yet another ilk of hovering parent who doesn't concede any independence to their child in terms of the vocation the child may want to pursue. There is inflexibility in their outlook about what the child should pursue, and they will try to ensure that their progeny follows the same path as them. So, if the father is a doctor, he may want his child to grow up with the constant reminder that she too has to become a doctor. So, she better 'choose' her subjects accordingly and work it all out backwards. It may be difficult for such a parent to concede to the fact that his child may have a strong passion for something totally different, such as the Liberal Arts. It is likely that the parent feels that it is unthinkable that his child could dream of following her own profession when the parent already has plans, like a family business to be pursued!

The 'You Must Achieve What I Could Not' Helicopter: I have known of a few young adults who graduated reluctantly to become engineers or doctors as per their parents' wishes, and soon found themselves feeling stifled in the wrong professional stream that was never their calling. In such situations, a youngster may either relent to his fate but remain frustrated and ungratified for the rest of his life, or change his professional stream midway (much against his parents' wishes), figure out his true calling and then, take off afresh in a completely different direction. This is a helicopter parent who wants to realize their failed self-aspirations through their young child.

But we often forget that instead of giving them wings to fly with, we as parents are smothering their dreams and aspirations by merely replacing them with our own dreams.

The 'You Can Do Better Than the Neighbour's Child' Helicopter: Many of us have felt anxious when we see another parent's child doing better than ours. And then one is likely to shift the gears of parenting a notch higher and start pushing the child harder. It is the child who starts to feel the anxiety and an enormous pressure. This ilk of parent succumbs to his peers' style of parenting. Seeing another parent do everything they can for their child, the parent with this mindset may feel that he may not be doing enough, and is likely to follow suit. While his intentions are well-meaning (as he just wants his child to do well), it's the insecurity that makes him anxious when he notices his friend's child doing really well in academics or in a sport, compared to his own child. Mostly, this anxiety is passed on to the child in a bid to motivate them to excel.

We need to be aware of the fact that every child is different, with a distinct developmental pace. Since this helicopter approach to parenting can be very counter-intuitive, we need to back off from hijacking the lives of our children, as this could sabotage their future. Your child may be better at something else, compared to other children, and you need to celebrate this uniqueness.

Parents who act out of peer pressure often feel very

disappointed when their children are unable to 'live up to their expectations'. Such parents are always very conscious that their children are being judged by their (parents') friends. So, they themselves may repeatedly resort to a lot of comparisons between their own children and those of their neighbours or friends. They will, in fact, do anything to give their children a competitive advantage over others, wherever and however they can. This approach to parenting can be very counter-intuitive.

What we often forget as parents is that there's indeed a marked distinction between being supportively involved in our children's activities and being in the driver's seat in their lives. If left unchecked, it can make way into our children's adulthood and is likely to affect their social and emotional growth.

Some reasons why parents may hover over their children:

1. The urge to protect the child from serious consequences of not excelling, such as not getting the desired job, not making it to a reputed team, their own unfulfilled dreams, etc.
2. The urge to overcompensate for the vacuum they felt during their own unloved and ignored childhood.
3. Peer pressure from other parents that can give a feeling of not doing enough for the child.

Here are reasons why you should avoid helicopter parenting:

While there is no harm in wanting the best in life for your child, taking away the reins of their lives from them can have serious consequences.

It robs children of innate coping skills: Children who are subjected to such overparenting, don't get a complete grip on their lives even as adults, as this type of parenting disempowers them. They are generally less competent, and lack independence and resilience. Problem-solving becomes a struggle for them, as hand-holding is all they've known. They live in the perpetual fear of dire consequences, which takes them further away from taking major decisions in life. They're vulnerable and sceptical, and live with the fear that the world is not a safe place to live in. This state of being can hamper a child's ability to succeed on their own steam, and can impair the quality of their lives considerably.

It can give them a sense of entitlement: Overprotection can make children 'me-centric'. They get used to having things their way all the time, and expect to have the best of everything in life without working hard for it. They are seldom grateful for what they have been bestowed with, because it all comes too easily to them from their parents' 'largesse'. These children face major difficulties in situations where things don't go their way.

It leads to anxiety and depression: Hyper-parenting can have a major effect on a child's mental and emotional well-being. They may always live under the fear of not being able to live up to their parents' expectations. The general home environment may become claustrophobic for them. They cannot enjoy any freedom to take their own decisions in life, and live in the constant shadow of their parents. Such children are very likely to experience anxiety and depression at some stage in life.[35-36]

It can lead to low self-esteem: When children with overprotective parents observe other children who have the freedom to take many small and big decisions of their lives, it may make them feel inadequate and incompetent. They may get the feeling that their parents don't trust their ability to be able to take decisions. This can lead to low self-worth.

It can impede their social lives: Overzealous parenting leads to unconfident children. They may turn awkward, self-conscious and become under-assertive in social setups. This can often lead to being jeered at by their peers, turning them into loners.

It can stunt cognitive development: The anxiety around trying to live up to parents' expectations can create undue pressure on them which is not conducive to intellectual growth. It can hamper their focus and attention span. This may lead to academic difficulties and falling grades. In worse cases, children are forced by parents to take up subjects they have no aptitude for, and the academic performance drops understandably.

So, how does a parent decommission their helicopter for good? If you find some shades of behaviour described above that match with your own parenting style, it would be a good starting point to acknowledge that to yourself. That would be the first step in alighting from your helicopter and thereafter, step by step, breaking it down and getting rid of it completely. You need to ease out of your unrelenting control on your child so that they learn to flap their wings and fly on their own.

How to let your child be:

Let them attempt age-appropriate tasks themselves: Tying a preschooler's shoelaces, combing his hair or making his bed is just fine, but doing all this for a teenager qualifies as hovering. Let your child attempt his tasks on his own, even if he struggles a little. Don't rush to salvage him at the first call for help for an uncomplicated job. This will get him into the habit of shirking from even trying. He is likely to succeed in a couple of iterations. But if he fails despite repeated tries, help him sail through.

Never impose rigid directives on them: Make suggestions, listen to their opinion, involve them in calm and meaningful discussions, and don't take major decisions on their behalf till they are convinced that it is the best decision in their interest. This approach will teach them to trust their own perceptions, a major step in the direction of making them independently thinking individuals.

Survey Takeaway: Kavya and Ashok Bhagat (from Agra) are the archetypal authoritative parents who exercised just the right amount of control on their two daughters (24 and 22 years old now) when they were younger. While they respected their girls' opinions and never imposed their will on them, they've been assertive in the right measure when the girls needed disciplining. They never set goals for the two, and gave them enough freedom to make mistakes, learn from failures and stand up stronger. Ashok recalls an incident from their elder daughter's school years. 'Mallika was nominated to become the head girl of her school, but eventually lost the election. She was appointed the social service leader instead. She was disappointed, and understandably so, as children take such things rather seriously at that age. We explained to her that what matters more is the fact that she was considered worthy of being the head girl, and that being the social service leader was as big a moment for the family as becoming the head girl would have been.'

Encourage them to express their views freely: It is important to encourage your child to think independently and express her points of view freely. Be respectful of her thoughts and consider them from the perspective of her age and maturity level. It will help her have a mind of her own.

Let them be accountable for their actions: Don't bail out your child from the consequences of her actions, unless the consequences are too harsh or unjustified, and you need to intervene to check their veracity. Your 'well-meant' meddling can leave her incapable of handling stress in future, when you're not around to pitch in.

Don't spoil them by never saying 'no': Don't bring up your child to think he is the centre of the universe. He shouldn't be raised to think that he will always have his way, and all his wishes will be fulfilled, however unreasonable or undeserving they may be. This can make him feel entitled, lazy, and always have expectations that others will chip in for him.

Encourage them to solve their problems themselves: Do not try to crease out every small and big issue your child faces. Encourage him to try and resolve his age-appropriate problems himself by thinking of various possible solutions. If he fails to come up with a solution, only then should you suggest ways of resolving the issue. But, never try to solve his problem without giving him a chance to come up with a possible solution and try it out.

Don't try resolving their relationship issues for them: Never commit the folly of managing your child's relationships with peers and others. This will leave her incapable of handling, sustaining and nurturing her relationships in future too. However, you can surely advise her if she seeks it from you.

Don't offer to complete their school projects for them: Avoid pitching in, even if your child is running out of time. This will not only make her lazy, but will also let her believe that it's okay to procrastinate and get such work done by you at the last moment.

Don't try to live your dreams through them: Do not try to make your child an extension of yourself by thrusting your dreams and aspirations upon him. He may not feel happy and fulfilled in the career path that you choose for him, or with the other life-changing choices you make on his behalf. Sometimes children may be in awe of or fear their parents too much, to be able to refuse to comply to their wishes, even if they feel stifled.

Alison Gopnik writes in her book, *The Gardener and the Carpenter* that there are two types of parents:

1. The 'carpenter' parent who follows a set of rules to reproduce something akin to the blueprint, thinks that a child can be moulded with specific interventions as per the blueprint of a 'perfect child' in their mind.
2. The 'gardener' parent who, on the other hand, provides a nourishing environment for the child's sustained growth, without really worrying about how different the child could turn out to be from most children of their age. There is no prototype in the parent's mind. This parent is ready to embrace the child with all their uniqueness.

Most modern parents are turning into 'carpenter' parents, while there's a dire need for them to be 'gardener' parents, whose primary focus is to nurture their children with love and care, without agonizing about how they will turn out to be finally.

So, while we need to put a blanket of safety around our

children and let them know we're always there for them, we have to nudge them out of their comfort zone to help them explore their distinct worlds to the fullest. A discerning parent would instinctively know when and how to 'let go'. They will not superimpose their will and ownership on their child, but help the child be his/her own person, unique in thoughts, opinions and feelings. This parent would also be aware that every child cannot possibly be exceptional at everything that they do.

Even if you are a carpenter parent, it is never too late to change. Just backpedal a little! You can start by slowly handing over the controls of your child's life back to her. This is likely to make her a stronger individual who can stand firmly on her own feet.

'Loving something for its own sake, not for its potential in fame or glory, is far from ordinary. It's an extraordinary blessing, a strength of character any parent would wish for their child,' says Kim John Payne in *Simplicity Parenting*.

10

Self-care for Parents

'The quickest way for a parent to get a child's attention is to sit down and look comfortable.'

LANE OLINGHOUSE, AUTHOR

LET'S ADMIT IT, parenting can be truly exhausting, even though it is rewarding. When I think of an overworked parent, I imagine a trapeze artist juggling balls while walking the tightrope. While the analogy may appear entertaining, the real predicament of a hassled parent is far from amusing. They are all wound-up and don't really know when a ball may fall, or when they might just miss one step during this balancing act and fall off the rope.

In a high-stress job like parenting, where even twenty-four hours a day seem precious little, it's easy to skimp on even the basic activities that can help the parent unwind a wee bit, like taking a slow warm shower or enjoying a hot and aromatic mug of coffee at a leisurely pace. The day just dissipates while they are busy getting the tiffin ready, rushing the children to the bus stop, getting the next meal ready, picking the children up from the bus stop, helping them with homework, driving them to their sports coaching, getting dinner ready, tucking them into bed on time; and the cycle repeats itself the next day. There seems to be 'no time for downtime'.

A parent who is the primary caretaker of the children and the home, is the backbone of the family. When they are stretched too thin, and scale near-epic levels of stress, there is a danger that they may just snap and break down. And what happens then? It can cause a lot of stress and tumult, and can disrupt the composure at home. To avoid this breakdown, the parent has to consistently invest time in their own personal upkeep and give priority to their well-being. They need to set aside a few hours a week for self-care, to re-energize themselves and breathe new life back into their being. This will help not only to recoup, but will also help to reclaim their daily responsibilities with renewed vigour.

If the mere thought of taking a break from your parental duties sends you on a guilt trip, you may be hurtling towards a setback of sorts. This burnout can have both short-term and long-term ramifications. These could be in the form of:

Physical malaise in the shape of hypertension, headaches, fatigue, low energy, frequent colds due to lowered immunity, etc.

Mental and emotional affliction in the form of agitation, moodiness, anger flare-ups, depression or feeling overwhelmed. This can rob you of patience, leaving you perpetually edgy and low-spirited. You may become a 'reactive parent', ready to blow your top at the first sign of a breach by the children.

Negative role modelling by teaching children that it's okay to neglect their well-being. By watching their parent remain perennially harassed, who never takes time out for self-care, children can start to think that this is how it is meant to be. They will never learn to respect and nurture themselves. They will view self-care as a guilty indulgence. And such an approach can seriously affect the quality of their life and future relationships.

Survey Takeaway: Hyderabad-based Agnes D'Cruz Rajesh, who is a mother of two boys (now 24 and 19 years old) would feel completely worn out in the early years of parenthood. She had forgotten that she was an artist, as all her waking hours were spent looking after the two boys and the house. She says, 'There came a point when I started feeling bottled-up and stressed. I desperately needed something to reboot myself. So, once my older son started school, I also joined his kindergarten school as the art and craft teacher. A couple of years later, when the pressure of multitasking was ready to blow me apart, I turned to painting as a hobby at home, and I made art a part of my activity even with the boys. So, it's been a win-win situation for all of us.'

Self-care is definitely not a selfish indulgence that you need to feel guilty about. It can, in fact, enhance your parenting skills by acting as a pressure-valve to release your day-to-day stress build-up. It will definitely help you approach your parental obligations with more buoyancy and enthusiasm, and children always love to have happy parents around them.

Top self-care ideas to help you reboot:

- Wake up late in the morning on the weekend, completely rejuvenated.
- Take a long, indulgent shower.
- Do a workout of your choice: outdoor yoga, Reformer Pilates, swimming, a contemporary dance class or a sport that you fancy.

- Make a healthy smoothie or a super-energising snack for yourself regularly.
- Get a comprehensive health check-up done annually.
- Get a full body massage or foot reflexology at a neighbourhood spa once in a while.
- Pamper yourself with a haircut, a pedicure or a hair spa at your favourite beauty salon regularly.
- Find time windows each week to read a book of your choice.
- Plan a film or dinner date with your spouse at least once a month.
- Schedule an hour a couple of times a month for a coffee or lunch date with a friend or a group of friends.
- If you treasure and long for 'quiet time' to reboot, just hang out at a coffee shop with yourself and a book to give you company.
- Watch a film with your spouse once in a while, and let your extended family or someone trusted take care of the children during those hours.
- Make time to listen to your favourite music.
- Set aside a couple of hours each week to pursue a hobby that you've been eyeing for long.
- Play a board game of your choice.
- Wear your favourite dress, get ready and step out—whether it is a special occasion or not.
- Go for a quiet trail walk amidst nature.
- Engage in some mindfulness activity, such as meditation, journaling or listening to meditation music.
- Call up a friend who always makes you laugh.
- Practise gratitude in your own way.
- Plant flowers if you haven't already. Gardening can be very soothing.

- Go window-shopping.
- Go for a long, quiet drive.
- Make a new friend.
- Do absolutely nothing and just lie in bed for a while, once in a while.

There can be numerous ways of indulging in self-care, and the ones listed above are just a few that came to my mind. These will not only replenish you and restore your lost cheer, but will have substantial pay-offs for your children too.

Remember, 'You can't pour from an empty cup. Take care of yourself first.'

Acknowledgements

My gratitude lineup will have to start with:

Charanjit Singh Sodhi (my husband): For you bore the brunt of my hysterics and rants caused by duress from writer's block (which was every so often). Much as you would've wished to (and understandably so) hurl me out of the tenth-floor window for being a niggling pest, you stumped me by displaying monk-like patience and being oh-so-zealous about my work! The book couldn't have seen the light of day if not for your relentless support.

Angad Singh Sodhi (my son): My heart beats for you so furiously that I often dread a cardiac arrest (too much love may be toxic!). My good fortune of landing the big project of being your mom lends the much-needed legitimacy to the parenting wisdom that I've doled out in the book. Your ludicrous capers every now and then, prodded me to caution the other parents and would-be parents that 'despite all your good parenting skills (or that's what you think!), your child can still end up in a loony bin!' Thank you, Angad, for your shenanigans that kept me from crumbling during those anxiety-ridden, low-creativity phases!

Maya (my house-help): You never lost your cool despite my persistent summons to supply endless cups of black coffee that you labelled as an unappetizing and non-nutritious dark liquid with a nauseating smell! Bravo for being an exemplary single mom to your young son. Your intuitive parenting prowess that I've come to discover from your unrelenting chatter, often leaves me awestruck!

Rupa Publications: For not dumping me after my first book and giving me yet again, a distinguished platform to share my insights about parenting with the world.

The Lord Almighty (the Infinite Spirit and the biggest author of them all): For endowing me with inspiration, ingenuity and self-belief which were imperative in bringing this book to fruition. I owe you everything!

References

1. https://beyou.edu.au/fact-sheets/development/emotional-development
2. https://www.verywellfamily.com/how-parents-fighting-affects-children-s-mental-health-4158375
3. https://indianexpress.com/article/parenting/health-fitness/parents-fights-effect-child-mental-health-and-behaviour-5384029/
4. https://indianexpress.com/article/parenting/health-fitness/parents-fights-effect-child-mental-health-and-behaviour-5384029/
5. https://www.bakadesuyo.com/2018/09/emotionally-intelligent-kids/
6. https://psychcentral.com/news/2018/11/11/too-much-screen-time-linked-to-anxiety-depression-in-young-children-and-teens/139931.html
7. https://www.sciencedaily.com/releases/2017/11/171114091313.htm
8. https://apps.who.int/iris/bitstream/handle/10665/311664/9789241550536-eng.pdf?sequence=1&isAllowed=y
9. https://www.healthline.com/health/piaget-stages-of-development#howto
10. https://www.ashford.edu/online-degrees/student-lifestyle/how-does-music-affect-your-brain
11. https://www.sciencedaily.com/releases/2014/06/140617211020.htm
12. https://parentslists.com/benefits-children-learning-instrument.html
13. https://clarketinwhistle.com/6584-2/
14. https://www.scanlonspeech.com/2013/05/15/how-arts-and-crafts-help-develop-language-in-young-children/
15. https://www.aap.org/en-us/about-the-aap/aap-press-room/Pages/American-Academy-of-Pediatrics-Supports-Childhood-Sleep-Guidelines.aspx

16. https://www.sciencedaily.com/releases/2019/05/ 190531135828.htm
17. http://citeseerx.ist.psu.edu/viewdoc/download?doi=10.1.1.905.3902&rep=rep1&type=pdf
18. https://www.ncbi.nlm.nih.gov/pmc/articles/PMC6123957/
19. http://www.earlyyearscareers.com/eyc/learning-and-development/supporting-speech-development-play/
20. https://www.climbingframes.com.au/kb/what-is-active-play/
21. https://www.psychologytoday.com/us/blog/freedom-learn/201001/the-decline-play-and-rise-in-childrens-mental-disorders
22. https://www.mayoclinic.org/diseases-conditions/depression/in-depth/depression-and-exercise/art-20046495
23. https://www.huffingtonpost.ca/tracy-gillett/reducing-teen-anxiety_b_12079974.html
24. https://kidshealth.org/en/parents/active-kids.html
25. https://health.gov/news/blog/2013/03/60-minutes-or-more-a-day-where-kids-live-learn-and-play/
26. https://www.ncbi.nlm.nih.gov/pmc/articles/PMC3905528/
27. https://www.webmd.com/mental-health/addiction/features/adult-children-of-alcoholics#1
28. https://www.medicinenet.com/low_self-esteem_may_lead_to_drug_abuse_in_boys/views.htm
29. https://www.psychologytoday.com/intl/blog/heartache-hope/201306/low-self-esteema-disposition-can-lead-addiction
30. https://www.ncbi.nlm.nih.gov/pmc/articles/PMC2792691/
31. https://www.ncbi.nlm.nih.gov/pmc/articles/PMC5615503/
32. https://www.pbs.org/newshour/economy/making-sense/money-habits-are-set-by-age-7-teach-your-kids-the-value-of-a-dollar-now
33. https://www.telegraph.co.uk/finance/personalfinance/10075722/Money-habits-are-formed-by-age-seven.html
34. https://www.moneymanagement.org/blog/2013/08/Do-your-children-know-enough-about-money.aspx
35. https://www.parents.com/parenting/better-parenting/what-is-helicopter-parenting/
36. https://www.psychologytoday.com/us/blog/when-your-adult-child-breaks-your-heart/201701/the-effects-helicopter-parenting

68